'Sorry, Boys, You Failed the Audition'

a novella

RAY CONNOLLY

Malignon

Copyright 2013 and 2019 Ray Connolly

Based on the BBC radio play
'Sorry, Boys, You Failed the Audition'
by Ray Connolly
First broadcast on 14 November, 2013

The moral right of Ray Connolly to be identified as the author of this work has been asserted in accordance with the Copyright, Designs and Patents Act, 1988.

All rights reserved. No part of this publication may be reproduced without the permission of the publisher.

Cover photo: Dezo Hoffman/Apple Corps Ltd

ISBN: 9781072290582

Find out more about the author at
www.rayconnolly.co.uk
mail@rayconnolly.co.uk

Malignon

Also by Ray Connolly

Novels
A Girl Who Came to Stay
That'll be the Day
Stardust
Trick or Treat?
Newsdeath
A Sunday Kind of Woman
Sunday Morning
Shadows on a Wall
Love Out of Season

Biography
Being Elvis – A Lonely Life
Being John Lennon – A Restless Life

Anthologies of Journalism
Stardust Memories
In the Sixties (edited)
The Ray Connolly Beatles Archive

Screenplays
That'll be the Day
Stardust
Forever Young (for TV)
Defrosting the Fridge (for TV)

Plays and Series for television
Almost Tomorrow
Our Kid
A Day In The Life
Honky Tonk Heroes (trilogy)
Lytton's Diary (series)
Perfect Scoundrels (series)

Documentaries for television
James Dean: The First American Teenager (writer-director)
The Rhythm of Life (co-writer of series)

Plays for radio
An Easy Game to Play
Lost Fortnight
Tim Merryman's Days of Clover (series)
Unimaginable
I Saw Her Standing There (short story)
God Bless Our Love
Sorry, Boys, You Failed the Audition
That'll Be the Day
Stardust

For Freda

This is a work of fiction. Although Freda Kelly was the Beatles Fan Club secretary for many years, this is not her story any more than it is theirs – and it obviously isn't theirs. So, my grateful thanks to Freda for allowing me to borrow her name and to invent a life for her that she hasn't lived…nor would have wanted to.

Author's Note

On January 30, 1969 John Lennon ended the Beatles' filmed concert on the roof of their Apple headquarters in London by joking: 'Thank you very much. We hope we passed the audition'. It was the last time the four would be seen playing together.

But what would have happened if six and a half years earlier, in the summer of 1962, the Beatles hadn't impressed at their all-important last chance to sign a record deal with Parlophone?

What would the future have held for John, Paul, George and Ringo if producer George Martin had said 'No'?

Chapter One

She'd always enjoyed the lunchtime sessions. It was the time the fans felt closest to them. There, with everyone stuffed together in the little barrel-shaped cellars, bodies slammed up tight in front of the stage, the more confident among them, always girls, would shout out requests. Whereupon John or Paul might acknowledge with a bit of friendly sarcasm. Just to be noticed in the crush could make a girl's afternoon.

Freda never missed those midday gigs, as typists from offices around the Pier Head, and messengers and clerks from the shipping offices along the Mersey, mingled with students down from the Art College. It was cheap, too, just one and sixpence to get in, and then a swift trade in Luncheon Vouchers for a roll and some tomato soup from the little café at the back.

It was the Cavern in Liverpool in the summer of 1962 – a warm, white cloudy day, and Freda was seventeen. And, as on the stage the Beatles were reaching the end of their set, she, the only-just-appointed fan club secretary, which, she was telling everybody, had to be the best job in the world, was excited. Not for herself, but for them.

The previous week the Beatles gone down to London and auditioned again for George Martin at Parlophone Records. It had gone really well, they'd thought, really well, and they were now waiting for Brian Epstein to come home with news of their recording contract. Brian had said it was a dead certainty they'd get one, so they were now rushing through the last song of the gig in anticipation of his arrival.

'All right, that's it, folks,' Paul McCartney was calling, even before the last chord had finished reverberating, as he lifted his Fender bass from around his neck. 'Thanks very much. Now off you go.'

'Yeah. Back to work, the lot of you. We'll see you tonight.' That was John Lennon, snapping bossily as usual.

'And without the curlers. All right, Helen?' Paul added, playfully chiding one of the regulars, a dolly redhead who liked to think her curlers wouldn't be noticed under her headscarf.

Helen, who always washed and set her hair on a Thursday night to be ready to go out after work on a Friday, blushed and giggled, thrilled to have been noticed again. Then she hurried off after her workmates.

Usually the Beatles would traipse across to the Punch and Judy Café at the entrance to Lime Street Station to meet their manager off the train after his trips to London, but he was coming to them this time.

'Any chance of getting a few autographs?' Freda asked, as the group unplugged their instruments. And, opening the file she was carrying, she took out some glossy eight-by-ten black-and-white photographs. With Ringo Starr only having replaced Pete Best on drums that week they'd had to have a new group photograph taken.

'Every chance,' George Harrison, the baby of the Beatles at nineteen, said, and, sitting down on the edge of the stage, held out a hand. 'Got any names to go with them, Freda...and a pen?'

Finding a biro in her handbag, Freda passed him a clutch of photographs. 'There's a Julie from Birkenhead. She wants one. Then there's Angela from Aintree...and all the girls from 4C at Seafield Convent. I think they'll have to share one. We haven't printed enough for the class to get one each.'

George started to sign the photographs. 'Convent girls? I like convent girls. Fresh ironing and toothpaste!'

'What?' Ringo had left his drum kit and was waiting for George to pass him a photograph.

'That's what they smell of... Convent girls. Peppermint and starch.'

'You'll wonder where the yellow went, when you brush your teeth with Pepsodent.' That was Paul, always ready with a song, even when it was only a jingle off the tele.

Behind them, John was watching the autographing.

'I'm more of a nun's man, meself,' he said.

'Oh, yes?' Paul passed him a photo and the biro.

'Especially those with dirty habits…'

'…and who ride old bicycles without crossbars,' Paul continued.

Ringo watched the exchange dolefully. 'I've never been out with a nun,' he said at last.

'Haven't you?' Paul feigned casual surprise. He and John were masters at straight-faced teasing.

'Shouldn't Brian be here by now?' George said, wandering to the staircase at the back of the club.

Paul looked at his watch. 'Any minute now…'

'If he hasn't been arrested for first class importuning in a third-class mail van,' John added, and returned to Freda the last of the signed photographs.

George ignored the comment. 'Do you think he'll bring it with him?'

'Bring what?' asked John.

'The contract. Is that how it's done in London?'

'Probably,' said Paul.

'Yes, with his cat and a cheese tied up in a red spotted handkerchief on the end of a stick, and a pocket full of gold he's scraped off the paved London streets.' That was John.

'Brian hasn't got a cat,' said Paul.

'I was being whimsical,' replied John

'You often are,' Paul answered

John turned to the fan club secretary. 'Well, it keeps out the cold, doesn't it, Freda?'

'Yes,' Freda agreed, though she hadn't really been following the chatter. It had just been Beatle-talk.

Ignoring them, Ringo put a hand to his ear. 'Aye-aye! Do I hear the tippy-tappy feet of...?'

'Our Eppy young manager about... time?' George finished for him, looking at his watch.

Freda approached the stairs as, rounding the corner of the stone steps, wearing a lightweight, navy blue summer suit, blue tie and shining leather soled shoes, her boss appeared. She smiled, pleased to see him.

'Welcome home, Brian,' said Paul.

'Hello, Boys...Freda...' Brian said quietly.

'How was London?' Freda asked. 'I think you got a bit of a tan.' She didn't quite know why she said that, other than that when anyone went away from Liverpool they almost invariably returned slightly pinker or darker, and everyone knew that London got all the sun while Merseyside got all the rain.

'Oh, I don't think...' Brian began to say.

But George interrupted: 'How soon do we start recording?'

'Yes. Have sticks will travel,' came in Ringo, tapping two drum sticks together like maracas.

Brian didn't answer.

'So?' Paul pursued.

'Sorry, Boys, You Failed the Audition'

'Brian cleared his throat. 'I'm sorry, Boys…'

'Sorry?' Paul questioned.

'No need to apologise. We are what we are.' John stung in jest – although it was still a sting.

'I meant to say… I talked to Parlophone and George Martin, and…I'm sorry, but you failed the audition.'

For a second nobody spoke. Freda thought she must have misheard.

'What?' Paul said.

'Failed…?' George moved a step closer to the manager.

'What do you mean?' Ringo asked.

'Failed? We were bloody brilliant!' John's voice was already raised in anger.

Freda looked at Brian. He seemed to have grown smaller, too, while he'd been away.

'George Martin was very nice. He said he thought you had potential. Lots of potential. And that he'd been looking forward to meeting your new drummer…' Brian glanced at Ringo…'

'But…?' Paul pressed.

'He's been over-ruled by the powers that be at EMI. Parlophone won't be recording you.'

There was a silence. In her few weeks in her new job, Freda had learned that Parlophone was the smallest and least important of the EMI group's record labels, the runt of the pack.

Brian tried again. 'I really thought that this time…'

'Christ, Brian!' John snapped.

'I don't believe it!' That was Paul.

'Did you tell him how big we are in Liverpool?' George wanted to know.

The manager sighed. 'He knows, but his bosses said that Liverpool isn't London!'

'It isn't Timbuktu, either!' John came back. 'Or perhaps it is to them in London. "Oh yes, Liverpool, a primitive little place on the sunny banks of the Khazi!" Bastards!'

Brian swallowed. He was shaking slightly.

'This isn't the end, though, is it?' Ever the optimist, Paul was looking for reassurance.

John turned on him. 'Bloody hell, Paul! How else would you describe losing our last chance? It's not exactly the beginning. Decca, Columbia, Philips, HMV…even Regal Zonophone… they've all showed us the door. It's like we're lepers. Nobody will touch us. Right, Brian?'

Brian didn't answer. For nine months he'd been telling anyone who would listen that the Beatles would be 'bigger than Elvis'. No-one had believed him, of course, especially not the Beatles themselves, but now he'd fallen at his first big hurdle. Even Freda knew that without a recording contract, the Beatles would be either condemned to stay in Liverpool, or, worse, have to emigrate to Hamburg, for the rest of their careers.

'Sorry, Boys, You Failed the Audition'

John recovered first. 'Well, that's it,' he said, swinging around. 'I can't stand here talking to you lot all day. I've got a pregnant woman to marry. I'll see you tonight' And he walked swiftly across the floor, and off up the steps.

Freda watched him go. She was astonished. Pregnant! His girlfriend, Cynthia was pregnant! Oh my God! She hadn't even known that they were…well, doing it! And they weren't even engaged.

George, who must have known, was already putting his guitar into its case. 'Even Brian Poole and the Tremeloes got a contract,' he said. And, without looking at Brian, he followed John out of the club. Freda knew what he meant. At the beginning of the year the Beatles had been down to London to audition for Decca, only to later discover that the company had signed the Tremeloes instead. Of course, they had. Brian Poole and the Tremeloes were a London group. Bloody London. It was always bloody London.

Ringo was the next to leave, after looking as though he was about to say something before changing his mind.

'It doesn't make sense,' said Paul at last. And, avoiding eye contact with Brian, he went, too.

Brian stared at the floor.

Freda tried to smile. 'I've er…I've typed the Newsletter,' she said.

There was no reply.

'It's ready for you to check.'

Brian seemed not to have heard.

'The Beatles Newsletter. It's finished...' Freda continued. 'But I suppose it might need a few changes now...'

'What?' Brian was struggling to concentrate.

'Well, I mean, the bit about the Beatles being...' Freda pulled the newsletter from her file and began to read... '"on the brink of becoming world famous recording stars and planning a nationwide tour and television appearances, with their new single to be followed by their first long player and a Hollywood film..." That's not quite the case now, is it?'

There were tears in her boss's eyes. She hated to see him like this.

'It's not your fault, Brian...' she said. 'I mean about Parlophone. Obviously not about Cynthia being pregnant.'

'They'll regret it,' Brian blurted.

'Oh yes, they will. They're too young. And she's still at college.'

'I mean Parlophone. They'll regret it.'.

'Oh! Yes! Parlophone! They're bound to.'

'When the Beatles are bigger than Elvis...'

'...they'll be kicking themselves.'

'As John would say...I hope they kick themselves to death.' And, with that, Brian turned and hurried away, back up the steps.

Freda looked around the empty Cavern. This wasn't how the afternoon had been supposed to end.

Chapter Two

There was no sign of Brian when she got back to the office. When he'd begun to manage the Beatles the previous December, he'd rented a couple of rooms over his family's NEMS record shop, just around the corner from the Cavern in Whitechapel; and Freda and Beryl, his secretary, had been given the smaller one. Today, presumably, not wanting to face anyone, he'd gone home to where he lived with his parents in South Liverpool, probably to 'bathe his psychological wounds'. That was the way Freda put it to herself. It was a phrase she'd noticed in a copy of Honey, which seemed appropriate for the moment.

Brian was an odd sort of fellow, quite posh really, a bit pompous, always very smartly dressed, and with a lovely Ford Zodiac, but somehow, although he was only 28, he seemed almost middle-aged. He didn't have a wife or girlfriend either, which struck her as surprising because he was really very nice, so it was upsetting to now see him looking so distressed. He lived for the Beatles. It must have hurt him to have let them down.

There were always chores to be done around the office, especially as Beryl was on holiday in Morecambe, so, for the rest of the day, Freda got on with putting the autographed Beatles photographs into envelopes, and answering the phone to a couple of new enquiries from Merseyside promoters wanting to book the group into local clubs. Similar requests came every day. How could the London record companies have turned down the Beatles when they were so good? Paul had been right. It didn't make sense.

Normally she would have gone home at half past five. But, as the Beatles were due to play an evening session back at the Cavern, after locking up the office, she went to the pictures to see *Carry On Cruising* at the ABC. Perhaps it was due to the mood she was in, but it really didn't seem very funny. Or perhaps it just wasn't very funny, anyway.

By the time she got back to the Cavern, the Beatles were on stage again and playing as professionally as ever, but, she thought, perhaps without some of their usual zest. Actually John, looked drunk, as he spat out the lines '*Give me money, that's what I want*'. She was glad Brian wasn't there to hear that. John could be very cruel when he felt like it.

Naturally, word of the failed audition had already got around the fans. 'It's a bloody disgrace,' Bob Wooler, the disc jockey who announced the acts, had growled on hearing the news. 'Typical of bloody, stuck-up Londoners.' But, though most Cavernites were similarly indignant

'Sorry, Boys, You Failed the Audition'

that Liverpool's best group had been rejected, some were relieved. Fame would have carried the Beatles away and not everyone wanted that. Even Freda was torn, but, as she knew very well, the Beatles wanted it desperately.

Normally, their sets ended on a high, with something like Twist and Shout, but tonight they were more subdued.

'I just want to thank you all for coming tonight,' Paul said before the last song. 'But, before we go, we'd like to do one more number. It's our hit record that never was, nor ever will be...' At which point John leant into the microphone with his harmonica in his hands and began to play the introduction to *Love Me Do*.

Her father was just switching off the television when she got home. There were just the two of them, and he worried when it got late, so she'd run all the way from the bus stop in Allerton to their semi-detached house in Canning Road.

To her surprise, he wasn't cross that she was late. Actually, he was smiling. Something had amused him. 'Well, Freda, you missed it tonight, all right,' he said as she was taking off her coat.

'Missed what, Dad?'

'Only the future.'

'The future? Really? Never mind. I'll catch up with it later.' Then, hanging up her coat on the bannister, she went into the kitchen and put the kettle on to make some cocoa. 'What future, anyway?' she asked as she returned to the living room.

'The Sixties future. On the television. A car driving along a road...'

'A car driving along a road is the future...?'

'In *America!*' Father rejoindered.

She didn't follow this. 'A car driving along the road in America is the future? Cars have been driving along roads in Liverpool for fifty years.'

'Halfway around the world it was, and we could see it here in England at the very moment that it was happening in America. It was as plain as... Well, to tell the truth, it wasn't very clear...'

'The horizontal hold slipping again, is it?'

Father ignored the interruption. 'But it was a historic moment, all right?'

'If not exactly the stuff of which legends are made.'

'Television all the way from America via something, well, a bit like a tennis racquet in the sky... That was what they said.'

'What? Where?' Joking, she went to the window, and, drawing the curtains, looked up into the night sky.

'You can't see it. I went out of the back door and looked all over...'

'For a flying tennis racquet. Are you sure you weren't watching *The Twilight Zone?*'

Father smiled. That was how they lived together,

always teasing and joking. He tried to explain. 'They aim the pictures into the sky in New York or Hollywood or somewhere and then an American Sputnicky thing bats them back down to Earth here in England.'

'It sounds like magic. Would you like some cocoa?'

'No, thank you. Magic to you and me, perhaps, but not to them. They call it Telstar and it's the future, I promise you. And you, young lady, were marked absent when it arrived.'

'I wasn't absent, Dad. I was with another kind of future. A musical one.'

'With those caterwauling layabouts in the Catacombs?'

'The Cavern, Dad. As you very well know. And they aren't layabouts.'

'But they do caterwaul. You'll admit that.'

Freda had to smile. 'Well, now and again, I suppose. When it suits the song. But it's you and the rest of the world who are missing the future, not me.'

Father got up from his chair. 'Just look at you, and you with a certificate of excellence in shorthand and typing. I don't know.'

'That's the trouble, Dad. You don't now. And neither does anybody else want to know.'

'I wish to Almighty God that you didn't either. Anyway, you get your drink. I've got an early shift tomorrow. I'll see you in the morning.'

'That'll be in the future then, will it?' Freda teased.

Father laughed. 'Goodnight. God bless.'

'Good night, Dad.'

And he stumped off upstairs to his bedroom.

Freda was thoughtful as she drank her cocoa. She'd read something in that night's *Liverpool Echo* about an experiment in satellite television, but it hadn't sounded like something that would encroach upon her life. The musical future was the only thing that interested her. But, had she been right when she'd said that the future was musical? She hoped so. She didn't think that the Beatles could face much more rejection.

Chapter Three

The hopes of high summer had all but collapsed by the autumn. The Beatles carried on playing in the Cavern and in other clubs and ballrooms around Liverpool, and Freda would loyally trek after them wherever they went, but it was clear to her that their enthusiasm was no longer there. When Brian had first become their manager, he'd enjoyed spending as much time as possible with them, usually taking them their pay on Friday nights. But that task had now begun to fall increasingly to her, and soon she found herself watching new tensions creeping into the way the boys treated each other. At first it was just that the jokes had become fewer, but then increasingly sarcastic and sometimes wounding comments began to surface. After that came the silences. She still hoped that Parlophone might change their minds as she wrote and posted items to the fans in the Beatles Newsletter, while Brian continued to make sure that road manager, Neil, and his assistant, Big Mal, got their petrol expenses punctually. But then, one night just before Christmas when the Beatles were playing a ballroom in Birkenhead, she saw how fraught things had become.

'All I'm saying…' Paul was insisting to John as Freda peeped in the half-open door of the dressing room, 'is that we haven't been writing much since the Parlophone set-back. And, if we don't come up with new songs of our own, we're just like any other group, playing the same old Chuck Berry and Motown stuff…'

'Which is great,' said John.

'But not *different*,' Paul insisted.

'And all *I'm* saying, Paul, is the only songs that audiences want to hear are those they already know. They look bored when we try anything new or that they haven't heard before. If we did only *Long Tall Sally* from now until kingdom come they'd be happy.'

'But *we* wouldn't. We'd be bored stiff. *You* more than anyone. We wouldn't get anywhere either.'

Freda glanced at Ringo and George. They were staying out of it.

'And I'm bored stiff with this conversation. You write if you want to, Paul. I'll write when I'm ready. All right! You can't just turn me on and off when you feel like it. I'm not a jukebox.' John's voice had risen to a rasp.

Turning away in frustration, Paul noticed Freda by the door. 'Ah, good ol' Freda…' he welcomed as she began to hand out the envelopes containing the group's pay.

John pretended to feel the thickness of his. 'I hope there's a Christmas bonus in here,' he grimaced. 'Cynthia's eating for five now.'

Escaping before the argument restarted, Freda made her way to the stage where Neil and Big Mal were setting up the amps and speakers.

'The trouble is, they're both right,' Neil explained. 'Apart from those who go to every single gig, fans do mostly want to hear hits. But you don't get hits of your own unless you make records.'

'Which the Beatles aren't able to do,' continued Mal.

'John likes writing as much as Paul,' Neil resumed. 'But, after playing together for so long...'

'This isn't how they'd imagined it would be,' Freda finished for him.

The Arctic arrived in Britain over Christmas. It was the coldest British winter of the century, the television said, and inevitably some Beatles appearances had to be cancelled. This was probably no bad thing, Freda decided, in that it gave everyone a little breathing space. So, when Brian called a band meeting at his office on January 2, 1963, in order to makes plans for the future, she was in high hopes. And getting there early to put the kettle on, she laid out a plate of the chocolate biscuits that Brian had asked her to buy. He always thought of little things like that.

John arrived first, wearing a big old tweed coat that she

knew had once belonged to his uncle, a woolly scarf and with mittens on his fingers. Then, practically ignoring her, he lay down on Brian's settee and began to draw something on a sketching pad. She knew better than to disturb him when he was being grumpy – as did the other Beatles, who arrived shortly afterwards, and who pretended not to notice his mood. Brian was last, beaming with New Year's delight.

'Good morning, boys and Freda. And a Happy New Year all round.'

'Happy New Year, Brian,' said Ringo.

George yawned and then apologised, saying that he'd been out for most of the night at a party in Bootle. Neither John nor Paul spoke.

Brian began the proceedings. 'Anyway, thank you for coming, on what they're saying is the coldest day on Merseyside since...' He stopped speaking, as if struggling to remember what he'd read in the previous night's *Echo*. The Beatles just stared at him.

'It said in the *Daily Express* that it's the start of a New Ice Age,' came in Freda, seeing her boss's discomfort. 'Apparently the world is getting colder and shipping in the Irish Sea will soon become hazardous because of all the icebergs...and there'll soon be penguins and polar bears in the Mersey, and ...' She paused for breath.

No one spoke.

'Anyone not want a cup of tea?' she asked quickly.

No hands went up, so one by one she passed around the mugs.

John stopped drawing when she reached him.

'What's that?' she asked, looking at his sketch.

'An upside-down tortoise,' he replied.

She should have left it at that, but found herself asking: 'Why is it upside down?'

'It was running for a bus on Upper Parliament Street this morning when it slipped on the treacherous New Ice Age ice, skidded down the pavement and flopped over on to its shell as it fell into the gutter, where it was pecked to death by a penguin or two and then trodden on by a short-sighted polar bear.'

'Oh,' said Freda. 'Is that enough milk for you?' And, after adding another drop, moved over to the window.

'Yes, well…' Brian said. 'As this is the beginning of another year, it seemed to me that it's time for a fresh start, and for us all to look ahead. Because I really think 1963 could be the Beatles breakthrough year.'

'That was what you said last year,' said George.

'I know. But I've got a good feeling about this year.'

'Okay,' Paul agreed. 'But if it is going to be our year, we're all going to have to try just a little bit harder.' He looked at Brian. 'Do you know what I mean?'

'Absolutely.' Brian had coloured slightly at the implied criticism.

'We can but try,' George mused philosophically.

'If at first you don't succeed, try, try and …' Ringo began.

'No,' interrupted John.

'No what?' asked Paul.

'No, what's the use?'

'What do you mean?'

'How long have we been doing this?'

'Five…six years.'

'That's longer than World War I, and no-one has noticed us.'

'That isn't true,' Paul protested. 'We've got hundreds of fans. Haven't we, Freda?'

Freda had the figures ready. 'Two hundred and twenty-two paid up member of the Beatles Fan Club, and we're currently waiting on thirty-five more who filled in the form but didn't send the postal order. I'm sure there must be a lot more, too, who put if off because they were saving up for Christmas.'

'And some in Hamburg, too,' Paul reminded.

'All right, a few in Hamburg,' John conceded. 'But nowhere else. It doesn't matter how hard we try, apart from them, no-one's listening.'

'Not yet,' Paul said,

John shook his head 'Not ever.' He paused. 'I've had enough.'

'Enough of what?' Ringo wanted know.

'Enough of no-one being interested.'

'Oh, come on,' Brian jumped in. 'Everyone has to weather some degree of disappointment when they're starting out.'

'This isn't the start, Brian. It's the end,' John snapped.

'The end of what?' Paul asked.

'Of rainbow chasing. If record companies are being run by tone-deaf turnips with marshmallows in their ears, I'm not going to waste any more of my life trying to be heard.'

Everyone stared at him.

'How *are* you going to waste your life then, John?' George finally asked lugubriously.

'I don't know, I'll think of something,' John said. Then, screwing up his doodle of an upside-down tortoise, he got up, buttoned his overcoat, wrapped his scarf more tightly around his neck, and left the office.

Ringo stared after him anxiously.

'It'll be all right,' Brian soothed. 'You know John. He'll be back.'

Freda glanced at Paul. He knew John better than anyone, and, suddenly, he looked very young.

There were only three Beatles at the Cavern the following night, with a member of the Swinging Blue Jeans standing in on rhythm guitar. And although Paul did valiantly as the sole lead singer, especially when he sang A Taste Of Honey – so well, in fact, that Freda wondered whether he might not one day make it on his own – there was no denying that the Beatles weren't the Beatles without John.

For the next few weeks the three-man group, aided by any available and semi-competent rhythm guitarist, soldiered on, hoping that John would have second thoughts and resume his place at the microphone. Then, one morning, Brian popped his head inside Freda's little office. His eyes were shiny.

'Paul phoned me last night,' he said quietly.

'Oh, yes?'

'Yes. He said he's given up waiting for John to change his mind and come back. He's decided to do his A-levels again. He wants to go to university.'

'*University?*' Freda was incredulous.

'He says his father is very pleased.'

Freda's heart went into free fall. 'Well, yes, I'm sure Mr Mac will be pleased,' she said. It was well known that Paul's father had worried for years that his elder son was in danger of throwing his life away hanging around with John Lennon. 'But where does that leave George and…?'

'Well, Rory Storm says he'll take Ringo back into the Hurricanes. They're going to Germany at the weekend for a tour of American Air Force bases. And George…he's looking around for another group.'

'Sorry, Boys, You Failed the Audition'

'Oh,' was all Freda could think to say.

'All of which means…,' Brian hesitated, embarrassed.

Freda stared at him. 'That the Beatles have…' She couldn't say the words.

'…broken up.' He finished for her.

'No,' Freda shook her head. 'They can't have. It's only 1963. It doesn't make sense.'

'But it's happened, Freda. And if the Beatles don't exist any more, I'm afraid they won't need…'

'A manager?' Freda said.

Brian smiled ruefully. 'Well, yes, that's true. They won't need a manager. But they also won't need…'

Realisation finally reached her. 'Oh, yes, a fan club…or a fan club secretary.' She looked at her boss. 'You're giving me the sack, aren't you, Brian.'

'I'm sorry, Freda.'

'So am I. But…what about you? What will you do now?'

Brian tried to smile. 'Oh, there's always the shop. I can still sell records even if I can't help get them made…' There was a catch in his voice, and he quickly continued. 'But I was right, you know. They could have been bigger than anyone ever, if someone had just given them a chance.'

'Yes. They would have been. And they should have been.' And, with that, Freda put on her coat, picked up her handbag and went home. She was too upset to do any more work that day.

'You'll soon get over it, love,' Dad sympathised. She was sitting at the kitchen table toying with her omelette, and he was getting ready to go to the football.

'I don't think so,' she said.

'Oh, yes, you're certain to.' He was wrapping a blue and white Everton scarf around his neck. 'But, next time, you want to make sure you get a proper job. With a pension.'

'A pension!' Freda gasped. 'I'm *seventeen!* What do I want with a pension?'

'You'll see. It comes around sooner than you think. Anyway, I'll see you later.'

'Yes, good luck. Hope they don't all play with both legs in one knicker again.'

She heard her father chuckling to himself as he went out of the front door.

She understood what he meant about getting a proper job. Security was everything to him. His generation hadn't been allowed to be young for long. He hadn't had any choice other than to grow up the minute he'd left school at fourteen. But it was different for her. She wanted to be young for as long as she could be, well, until she was really old – twenty-nine, at least. Dad couldn't understand that. But then, there'd never had anything like the Beatles in his day.

She reflected on the first time she'd seen them, as she

washed the dishes. She'd just left secretarial college and had been at her first job in a typing pool when a girl called Pauline in another office had dragged her off to Mathew Street one lunch hour. She'd wondered where she was going, as they'd gone down the thirty-three steps, and then squeezed into the little club under a fruit and vegetable warehouse. But then she'd heard them and, pushing through the crowd, seen them, up on that tiny Cavern stage. Their faces had been shining through the fug of sweat and music and she'd been transfixed by the clashing of guitars, the John and Paul harmonies, the arrogant sarcasm of the one and the romanticism of the other. And her life had changed.

The song had been *I Saw Her Standing There*, and when Paul had sung, 'She was just seventeen, you know what I mean' she'd felt as though it was about her. People in show business were usually glamorous, or phoney American spivvy types who wore natty, shiney suits and talked posh, or even worse, like Londoners…Cockneys. But the Beatles had been boys who talked like her and thought like her.

It hadn't just been about her fancying them, either. Well, yes, sometimes she'd wondered if she would have had the willpower to say 'get off' if one of them had ever tried it on. She knew she wouldn't, obviously. She wasn't daft. But that was never going to happen. Paul and George weren't much older than she was, but they weren't meant for girls like her – although other, more pushy girls, had their fantasies. She was in love, yes, not with the Beatles as individuals, but with the idea of them, their cheek and youth, their wit and jokey insolence, their music, and the sheer joy they invoked in their audience. Something happened in the Cavern when they were there, something she could relate to more than anything in her life.

These weren't polished-until-they-shone, far away creatures off the television, but flesh and blood young men who, on that stage, seemed to be stars before they were stars. She'd never experienced anything like their sheer exuberance. But, more than that: they'd been so *Liverpool*, and so *good*.

With them in her life, being young in this backwater of a northern port had come to mean being at the centre of the entire universe, in touch with a new generation in a way her father couldn't begin to imagine.

And now that the Beatles had broken up, she couldn't imagine life without them.

Chapter Four

Getting to work early the following day, she found Brian already removing the Beatles Cavern posters that he'd had stuck on his walls. She came straight to the point. 'If it's all right with you, Brian, I'd like to keep the Beatles Fan Club going.'

He looked puzzled. 'I'm sorry, Freda. But as I'm getting out of management, I'll be giving up the office.'

'I won't need an office. I can do it from my bedroom. And I won't need paying either.'

Brian considered her kindly. 'But there'll be nothing for you to do. With no Beatles there'll be no fan letters to answer or photographs to get autographed…no signatures to fake…no bookings to chase or appearances to announce.'

'I know. I know. But I can't help thinking it will be a terrible shame if, just because they never made it, the Beatles are forgotten and no-one in fifty years' time has ever heard of them or knows how wonderful they were. I can't let that happen.'

Then she got on with helping Brian wind up his part in

the Beatles' careers, before, at lunchtime, going to the Post Office down the street where she withdrew twenty pounds from her savings account. It was money that she'd been saving for a rainy day, but days didn't come much bleaker than this one. Going over to a second-hand typewriter shop in Dale Street, she chose an old reconditioned Underwood that came with two spare ribbons. It was heavy, and she felt as if her back and arms were breaking as she carried it to, and then from, the bus, and then home, and up the stairs to the dressing table in her bedroom.

'Now what?' her father asked, when, getting back from work, he heard the tapping of the keys and came upstairs to investigate.

'Just a hobby,' she said, and shoo-ing him out, she re-read a stencilled newsletter she'd written to all the two hundred and twenty-two Merseyside fans on her Beatles Fan Club mailing list.

> *'Dear Fellow Fans*
>
> *'I know you'll have heard the terrible news by now. Yes, they've broken up. It's heart-breaking, isn't it. But, don't worry. Starting today, I'll still be keeping you up to date with everything John, Paul, George and Ringo are doing by way of this Ex-Beatles Fan Club Newsletter for as long as you want to read about them.*
>
> *All the Beatle best.*
>
> *Freda'*

'Sorry, Boys, You Failed the Audition'

Then she wrote to all four, now former Beatles, asking them to keep her in touch with their news.

She went to Brian's office for the last time the following morning, and watched as the Gestetner machine ran off her first newsletter. As a farewell gesture, he gave her the envelopes and paid for the stamps. Then, with her mail-out posted, she made her way to an employment bureau in Bold Street.

By the time she got home that night she had a new job as a shorthand-typist in a solicitor's office. Her father was very happy. At eight pounds a week, it was a steady job in, what he called, a reputable profession.

As she'd expected, reaction from the fans to her newsletter was immediate, and while several welcomed her enterprise, more than a few wrote to say they'd felt abandoned by the turn of events. Not altogether surprisingly, there was no response from the ex-Beatles themselves. They, it appeared, had already moved on.

Freda was undismayed. She knew her city. While Liverpool may look big on a map, the centre is really quite small, almost village-like, and soon information about the four was finding its way to her from friends, fans and the group's relatives. Paul, she heard through his brother Michael, who was a trainee hairdresser at the new André Bernard salon, was now studying hard, having even been accepted back at his old school, the Liverpool Institute. That's Paul, she thought, always busy and ambitious.

John, on the other hand, was said to be doing very little apart from drawing his cartoons of ugly people for the local pop music newspaper *Mersey Beat*, while he and Cynthia awaited the arrival of their baby in two rooms of bohemian squalor near the Philharmonic Hall. That seemed typical, too. John only had two speeds. Full out and full stop.

So, with Ringo beyond reach, drumming in West Berlin with Rory Storm, the main item in Freda's next newsletter was about George. He'd found a new band to play with – the Pete Best Five. Their first gig was on the Royal Iris as it ferried up and down the Mersey. She was there, of course.

'It's very kind of Pete to take you on, isn't it, considering you broke his heart when you and the other Beatles sacked him in favour of Ringo,' she told the guitarist more bluntly than she'd intended when he popped outside on deck for a cigarette during the interval. 'It's lucky he doesn't bear a grudge.' She'd become very fond of Ringo, but she'd always thought that Pete had been shabbily treated.

George smiled nonchalantly as they passed the lights of New Brighton. 'There've been a lot of riffs played since then, Freda. I'm a guitarist. I'll play with anybody who asks me. Perhaps I'll be with another band next month or next year. Who knows? Just as long as I can play.'

'*I suppose that's how it is with musicians,*' Freda typed

when she got home. '*Loyal only to the music. It's more personal for us fans, isn't it? We can't chop and change our loyalties as the mood takes us.*

Which reminds me, John was spotted with Cynthia pushing a crying baby in a second-hand pram along Otterspool Promenade last Sunday morning. I never imagined John as the baby-walking type. So, it's congratulations to John and Cynthia. And, oh yes, thanks to Nigel in Crosby who's written to report that Paul has got a conditional offer of a place at university in London. He would, wouldn't he? I hope he doesn't go all la-di-da like everybody else who goes down there.

All the Beatle-best.

Freda.

PS Keep the news coming!'

The sound of her father's quiet tread on the stairs sounded as she pulled the stencil from her typewriter.

'You still working, love?' he said as he pushed open the door and sat down on the end of her bed.

'It's not work,' she said.

'No, but…this Beatles thing you're doing… Promise me you won't waste too much of your time on it. You want to get out and get over it. Meet some new people. Get a boyfriend.'

She sighed. 'I'm not wasting anything, Dad. And I don't want a boyfriend. He'd only be a pest anyway. They always are.'

'And the Beatles weren't?'

'No.' She tried to explain. 'It isn't only about the Beatles. It's about us, too, all the Liverpool kids who followed them. The Beatles gave us a kind of hope.'

Her father raised a weary eyebrow. 'Hope?'

'Yes. Hope. When we thought they were going to be stars we all felt good because we'd recognised them first and helped them get started. So, it was like our start in life, too.'

'In a dingy cellar smelling of rotten fruit and disinfectant?'

'And worse,' Freda laughed. 'Jesus was born in a stable. That wouldn't have smelled very nice either, would it? But look how famous he became.'

'Now, now,' her father chided. 'He hears every word.'

Freda glanced upwards. 'Sorry, Jesus. No offence. But…'

'Yes?'

'Well…because of the Beatles, other people in the Cavern had their dreams, too…the Searchers and the Merseybeats and the Fourmost. Everything began to seem possible for everybody. Even the girl who works in the cloakroom. She dreams about being a singer and a star on the tele…'

'Can she sing?'

'Cilla? Well, if you like that sort of thing. But Gerry

Marsden can. Him and the Pacemakers do something about walking on and on through a storm with hope in your heart and never being alone, and it's really moving.'

'You don't mean that song from Carousel, do you? You'll Never Walk Alone.'

'I don't know. Is that what it's called.'

'I think it might be. Joseph Lock sang it just after the war. Your mother used to like it, God bless her.'

'Really? Well, anyway, it's like a hymn. And that's how I feel sometimes, walking through a storm but getting there in the end. But, you know, Gerry's always been a few laps behind the Beatles, and if they can't make it, well, Gerry's got no chance, has he? Which means no-one will ever hear him singing it, or know how inspiring it can be. The Beatles were the best by miles. But if they can't make it, nobody else from Liverpool will either.'

Father got up. 'You're a funny girl. Loyal as a limpet. But, come on, put the Beatles away now, or you'll never be up for work in the morning. Goodnight.' And, kissing the top of her head he went off to bed.

Chapter Five

With her days at the solicitor's office now filled with probate and conveyancing, and her evenings spent either at the pictures or at night school on an introductory law course, life was busy for Freda. It wasn't, however, terribly exciting any more. How could it be? Extraordinary headlines about prostitutes and politicians involved in the Profumo Affair, the audacity of the Great Train Robbery and the assassination of President Kennedy might have filled the newspapers, but with the charts dominated by an Australian yodeller called Frank Ifield, it seemed to Freda that, musically, Britain fell asleep.

Her weekend routine, like almost every other young person in the country, was to lie in bed until ten o'clock, and then go downstairs in her dressing gown and listen to the BBC's teenage show, Saturday Club, on the radio. Which is exactly what she was doing when one morning in December, just as she was settling into her tea and toast, the door bell rang. She went to answer it.

'Hi, Freda! Looks like you've got some Chrissie cards

from your never-say-die Beatle fans.' A smiling, good looking student, wearing a navy-blue duffel coat and striped college scarf, his trousers in bicycle clips, was holding out a wad of envelopes.

'Paul!' Freda gaped.

'*Please, Mr Student Christmas Postman* to you, young lady, in your Huckleberry Hound carpet slippers and cosy dressing gown.' Paul smiled. 'How *are* you? I hear you're soliciting now.'

'I work in a solicitor's office, if that's what you mean,' she said, feeling a little put-out by his condescension, and desperately wishing he hadn't caught her before she'd done her hair. 'I hardly recognised you.' Nor had she. Paul the student looked nothing like Paul the Beatle. 'Do you want to come in for a cup of tea? I thought you were still in London.'

'Well, just for two minutes,' Paul agreed, and followed her into the house. 'But, no tea, thanks. Term's finished. I'm doing the Christmas post like all the other students.'

'Oh, right,' she said. '*Like all the other students*' sounded a bit show-offy to her. She looked at him. He was now dressing the intellectual part. 'Are you in a group down there?' she asked. That was what really interested her.

Paul laughed. 'You're supposed to ask me what I'm studying. Actually, they don't like rock music where I am. They think that it's music for the mindless. They're into trad jazz.'

'No.' She was shocked.

'Honest. I have to hide the *New Musical Express* inside the *Guardian* or they'll think I'm thick.'

'There's a bloke in our office hides *Woman's Own* inside the *Football Echo*. He likes the knitting patterns.'

'It takes all types.'

'Yes. Doesn't it. You are still playing your guitar, though, aren't you? At college, I mean,' she pursued.

'Well, yes, in my room. I've got a bedsitter in Bayswater. But mainly I write tunes for the drama society to put topical lyrics to. Everyone's mad on satire since *That Was The Week That Was* came on the tele.'

'Oh, nice,' she said, without enthusiasm. 'I bet John would be good at writing satire.'

'John would be good at anything he put his mind to,' came the brusque reply.

'Have you seen him since you've been back?'

'No.'

'But you wrote to him from London?'

'No.'

'You should. And you should go and see him. He's writing funny little short stories now. Did you see the one in *Mersey Beat*?'

'They don't sell *Mersey Beat* in London,' Paul said rather loftily.

'Don't they?' She was astonished. 'It's great. There was

a page of his drawings, too. He even got one in the *Echo*.'

'Well done, John.'

'Yes, well done.' She hesitated, unsure of what to say next. 'Would you like some toast?' she offered.

'Thanks, but, I'd better be getting on...' He began to leave.

She was anxious to prolong the moment. 'So...?'

'Yes?'

'Well, I mean, is there anywhere as good as the Cavern in London?'

He frowned. 'It's different. I've been to a couple of clubs in Soho ...the Marquee and the Scene. I saw one group that was all right. They're a bit bluesier than we used to be, but they're not bad. They're called the Rolling Stones. They might make it.'

That's a phony name for a group, Freda thought. But she said: 'No group could ever be as good as the Beatles.'

Paul shrugged: 'No...well, that's what we used to think, too. But it wasn't to be. Anyway...' He was already in the hall.

'You're all dead mean, you know,' she suddenly said.

'What? Why'

'Well, here I am running the Ex-Beatles Fan Club and Newsletter, and we've got members desperate to know whether you've got a cough or a cold or a new hairstyle, which you obviously have, or a different guitar...even a new plectrum or drum stick would do. But not one of you ever bothers to get in touch and tell me anything.'

Paul sighed. 'Freda, it's finished. The Beatles were then. We're all now. And you should be, too. I wish it had turned out differently, but what's past is past. It wasn't meant to be. I'm sorry.' He opened the front door. 'Anyway... I have to finish my round. Happy Crimble.' And, with that little reminder of John, who'd invented the phrase, he was out of the door and swinging his leg over his Post Office bicycle.

Freda watched unhappily as he cycled on to the next house. 'Happy Crimble, Paul,' she muttered to herself as off he went without a care. He didn't know what it was like to be a rock and roll orphan. How could he?

Going back into the living room, she began to open the Christmas cards and put them on the mantelpiece. Paul should have kept them for his fancy bedsitter in London, she mused. They were mainly for him. And George of course. The good-looking ones in any band always got the most fan letters...and offers of other favours, too.

What was that he'd said about some bluesey group he'd seen, she tried to remember. They might make it, he'd reckoned. Well, Paul was usually dead right about everything, but he was going to be dead wrong about whatever the London group was called. He'd obviously been away from Liverpool for too long. He was losing his mojo.

Chapter Six

Her first grown-up holiday took her with her friend, Judy, to a Butlins Holiday Camp in North Wales the following summer. It was a favourite spot for young Liverpudlians, and well known for chalet romances, too, but the poster of Ringo that greeted her in the reception area came as a surprise.

In his short time with the Beatles, Ringo had been the new one at the back, the one of whom nobody had expected very much other than a steady and more adaptive beat. But since the break-up he'd been the busiest of them all, hardly ever at home in Liverpool as he'd at first toured with Rory Storm. Now he even had his own band, Ringo's Raiders.

Obviously, she went to see them on her first night there. With his collarless French jacket, and the spotlight on him for his drum solos, which were mercifully short, because there wasn't much Freda hated as much as drum solos, he was a star…a Butlins star, anyway. So, she found herself feeling honoured to be sitting with him and Judy in the Welsh Rarebit snack bar the following morning.

'I know we're not particularly creative,' he admitted as, sheltering from the relentless North Wales rain, they drank frothy coffee. 'But the money's good and every week the bus brings a new flock of girls to fall in love with. Who could ask for anything more?'

'John and Paul…' she began to say, and then stopped herself, when Ringo shook his head.

'John and Paul…stubborn isn't the word. That's the trouble when you have two lead singers who write the songs as well. When they fell out the whole thing collapsed. In my band I'm the boss. It makes everything a lot easier.'

And, as a different record came on the juke box, he joined in the rhythm with his spoon on his empty cup. It was the Rolling Stones' *It's All Over Now*.

Freda frowned. She'd been at the holiday camp for less than 24 hours and she must have heard this bloody record twenty times already. Paul had been right, after all, when he'd told her the Rolling Stones were good, but even he hadn't predicted that Stones hysteria would sweep the country, or warned her about the funny little singer with the tiny hips, mincing steps and big lips.

'If Mick Jagger dared ponce about in the Cavern the way he does on the tele, he'd be chucked in the Albert Dock,' she said as Ringo listened to the record.

'They say he's the face of Young London,' the drummer countered pleasantly.

'Which tells you everything you need to know about

London, doesn't it?'

Ringo gave her a worldly-wise smile. 'Are you sure that isn't a little bit of envy leaking out?'

'Of course, it is. And it's flooding out. All the time. All over the place. I'm knee deep in it. You should be, too.' She wasn't ashamed. She was just fed up with reading how the Rolling Stones were the 'Pied Pipers of a new generation' and that everything that was exciting was happening in London. It was as if nowhere else in the world existed.

She went to see Ringo's Raiders every night for the rest of her holiday. They were good enough, doing mainly the latest hits, but they weren't the Beatles.

She didn't get off with anybody. Not properly. Although Judy did. She always did. That was what holidays were for, she liked to say. Freda was a bit more choosey.

If she felt left out of the excitement that the Rolling Stones were generating, it must, she was certain, be murder for Brian Epstein. He didn't come down to the Cavern any more, but she would see him sometimes in the window of his family's shop, as he arranged displays for records by Sandie Shaw and Helen Shapiro.

'I'm enjoying reading about my former clients in your Ex-Beatles Newsletter,' he beamed on Saturday morning as, outside on the pavement viewing his shop window, he spotted her passing.

'Really? Thanks.' She was flattered.

'And the fans… still loyal?' Brian enquired.

She hesitated. 'Well…the froth always floats off first, doesn't it,' she said, not wanting to admit that some of them seemed a lot less keen than she did. 'But the true believers…they're still there.'

'And the Beatles? Still not co-operating?'

She shook her head. 'According to Paul's dad, he's gone grape picking with some college friends at a vineyard in the South of France for the summer.'

Brian smiled. 'That's Paul.'

'Yes,' she agreed. 'I've never known anyone from the Cavern go grape picking. Potato picking at half-term in the fields beyond Aintree, but grape picking…? Never.'

'Ever the romantic,' Brian decided. 'Did you know that George popped in the shop the other week looking for strings for his guitar. He's doing all right.'

'Yes. But I bet he didn't tell you he backed Cliff Richard in Wolverhampton when Hank Marvin had a wart on the end of his thumb.'

'No?'

'Yes. I suppose that made him temporarily almost semi-famous by association, didn't it? He tried to keep it a secret, so I didn't put it in the newsletter. It didn't seem fair. He'd never dare show his face in the Cavern again if it got around that he'd played with Cliff.'

'That was very nice of you. But what about John

'Sorry, Boys, You Failed the Audition'

throwing Cynthia's mum's television into the Mersey? Was that true?'

Freda laughed. 'I couldn't resist it. The story I was told was that Brian Poole and the Tremeloes were on *Ready, Steady, Go* and John just couldn't take it. It was a brand-new telly, too. A big, 13-inch screen, and not even paid for.'

'I know. She got it in our shop. She had to buy another. It's an ill wind, Freda.'

'Isn't it just? But that's John. The centre of attention when he isn't even there.'

For months the gossip had been that John's main occupation was writing mainly unpublished little poems and stories. But from what Freda had observed it seemed to be more a case of him nursing a cappuccino or pint and making people laugh, as he held forth comically about his misfortunes. Friends said he was turning into a local wit and should be on the tele. Others, less well disposed, reckoned he got his best laughs when he went to collect his dole money at the Labour Exchange after his Beatles' savings ran out.

He'd always been funny, even when he wasn't being very nice, so perhaps he would one day end up being a famous comic, Freda would sometimes think. It was certainly possible. On the other hand, without Paul's hard work and discipline, he might just…end up.

In the meantime, although the ex-Beatles continued to blithely disregard her efforts, she was never offended and continued with her newsletter. They just didn't get it, she would tell herself. And, although not invited to Ringo's wedding to his girlfriend, Maureen, she skilfully coaxed the details from his mother. And when Mr McCartney told her of Paul's success in his university exams, she expressed her congratulations in print.

She was the perfect fan. But it broke her heart that they'd broken up before they'd made any records, because, while Rolling Stones' fans could listen to their favourites every hour in the day, Freda only had memories.

Chapter Seven

It was lashing with rain as she stepped out of the solicitor's office in Whitechapel and set off scurrying down the pavement. It had been a bright, sunny day when she'd asked, and been given, permission to take the afternoon off work. But the weather had turned, and, by the time she reached the cobbled alleyway and the shelter of the Cavern, she was soaked. Making her way down the steps, she could feel water running in rivulets off her hair and down on to the shoulders of the new summer jacket that she'd bought for the occasion. It didn't seem fair. She'd done her hair specially the night before. Now she was going to look a mess on the big day.

Jenny and the Cortinas were on the little stage singing *Baby Love* as she entered the club, with all three wearing the shortest skirts Freda had ever seen. Perhaps they didn't sound as good as Diana Ross and the Supremes, but, considering the sparsity of the audience, they were snappy enough. The weather hadn't done them any favours, either.

Spotting her arrival, Jenny began to end her set, and, as

Freda tried to dry her hair with a towel, the Cavern's disc jockey, took to the microphone.

'Thank you, Jenny and the Cortinas, for another wonderful display of...well, display! It's always good to welcome you back. And now, as Cilla puts the sausage rolls in the oven to warm, we're ready for this afternoon's main event ...the 1965 Ex-Beatles Fan Club Annual Convention. So, can I have a big hand for the president, secretary, editor and intrepid newshound of the Ex-Beatles Fan Club Newsletter, without whom none of us would have got soaked coming here today... Without more ado and a-don't, over to you, our ever-faithful Cavernite...Freda...' And he passed Freda the microphone.

A scattering of light applause welcomed her as Freda cleared her voice. 'Hello, everybody, and thank you for bracing the rain today. It's lovely to see you all again.' She hesitated, then summoned up her courage. 'But, before I go any further, I have some disappointing news for you. I had hoped that George, as in Harrison, would be joining us. But I've just been told by his mother that he's been asked to help out as an extra guitar with the Moody Blues in Billericay tonight. I'm sure he'll be as disappointed as we all are that he couldn't be here with us.'

A murmur of dismay resonated in the cellar, followed by the sound of a couple of lads leaving.

Freda pushed on. 'I had hoped to get Ringo as a replacement...' she said, not entirely truthfully, 'but he and

'Sorry, Boys, You Failed the Audition'

Maureen seem to have disappeared since they got married. It's a bit of a mystery actually. So, if anyone knows where I can find him...?'

She looked around. Expressions remained blank. Nervously, she began again. 'Anyway, wherever Ringo is, I know that he and George, as well as Paul and John, will be pleased that, with your help, I've managed to complete a list of everything the Beatles ever played...and which I'll be sending out with the next newsletter...together with the names and dates of every club they ever played in.'

Judy and a couple of other loyal friends clapped, but without any enthusiasm.

'Thank you,' Freda said. 'It's really quite interesting.' Then, stoically, she began to read the list of venues...

Dad was setting the kitchen table when she got home, wet and unhappy.

'You can't really blame them, love,' he said as he took her coat and hung it over a maiden by the fire. 'It's a terrible day to be out.'

'But that isn't why people are losing interest,' Freda confessed.

Her father hesitated as he seemed to ponder the kindest choice of words. 'Perhaps a fan club for a group who never got anywhere...and who no longer exist wasn't your best idea,' he said at last.

She didn't answer, so he continued setting the table,

then brought a bowl of chips and a plate of fish fingers and set them down with a pot of tea.

'They say that Ken Dodd is doing very well in the pop charts,' he remarked as they began to eat.

'Yes,' Freda agreed.

'He's very popular.'

'Yes.'

'So… perhaps you should do a fan club for him instead of the Beatles.'

She looked up at him. 'For Ken Dodd?'

'He's very funny.'

'I know. But he's a middle-aged comedian with fuzzy hair, sticking out teeth and a tickling stick.'

'That's true. But he can carry a tune.'

'It wouldn't be the same.'

'No? Oh well, it was just a thought.'

They went back to their dinner.

'What about the Permissive Society then?' Father suddenly asked.

'That isn't a group.'

'Isn't it? They're always going on about it in the papers. It sounds like one, don't you think?'

'Perhaps a London group. But I can't see anything called the Permissive Society ever catching on in Liverpool.'

'And thanks be to God for that.' And her father smiled.

49

She had to laugh. 'You are rotten.'

'Not really,' he said. 'I'm just a dad, worrying that his daughter is throwing her young life away on a memory.'

'But I'm not, Dad. And I'm fine. Honest.'

'Honest?'

'Honest.'

'Good girl. So, will you have another fish finger? Fresh today. I caught it myself this morning.'

Chapter Eight

The World Cup finals reached Liverpool in July 1966, the month Freda found herself wearing a bridesmaid's dress for the first time. To no-one's surprise, her friend Judy had discovered that she was pregnant, but when word reached Freda from a guest at the wedding reception that John Lennon had, at last, sold a comedy sketch to BBC Television, that was unexpected, and almost exciting. Unfortunately, the programme *was* due to be broadcast when Portugal were playing the diddy-men from North Korea, as Liverpudlians had christened them, at the Everton ground in a match that was going to be televised,

'*Dear Fellow Fans,*' Freda wrote in a hurried newsletter, '*I hope some of you can manage to tear yourselves away from the World Cup to see John's sketch on the Spike Milligan Show on BBC-2 on Saturday.*

He's been scribbling and doodling away ever since you know what… and finally he's got his first national success - even if it is only two minutes long.'

In truth, when she saw it, she thought it was silly rather

than funny. But she was thrilled to see his name on the screen, and wrote a letter to him in congratulations.

She received a postcard almost by return of post. It showed a gorilla reading a Bible. On the back John had written:

> *'Dear Freda, As Hamlet's step-father almost said: "My words fly up, my thoughts remain below. Girls without knickers never to heaven go."*
>
> *Love to you and yours*
>
> *From me and mine*
>
> *John.'*

What knicker-less girls had to do with anything – apart from the obvious – Freda didn't know, but she saved the card anyway. If John ever did end up famous it might be valuable one day. You never could tell with John.

You never could tell with George either. He'd always been the quiet one, giving her a lift home from the Cavern in the first car he'd owned, and never saying much. But he seemed to be coming out of his shell as he moved around the country helping out one band after another. Too ambitious to stay long with the Pete Best Five, he'd become a freelance guitarist for hire, playing on a couple of Troggs' recordings and even sitting in on a session with Manfred Mann. He was going places, if only in little steps.

So when, on coming out of work one night, Freda

noticed in the *Liverpool Echo* a caption under a photograph of a tanned, bottle blonde with a beehive, wearing a white swimming costume and high heels, that announced that '*Miss New Brighton 1966*' had become engaged to '*musician George Harrison*', it was her duty to investigate. She hurried to a phone box in Exchange Station and phoned George's mother.

'You've just missed him, love,' Mrs Harrison explained. 'He's gone over to his allotment.'

Freda thought she must have mis-heard. 'His what?'

'His allotment. He was worried that the wind might have ruined his hollyhocks while he's been away. Hasn't the weather been awful!'

'Hollyhocks?'

'Yes. He's become very keen on gardening. Didn't you know?'

'Er, no. I didn't know. But…' She stopped. None of this sounded quite right.

'Yes?'

'Well, I mean … George is a rock and roll guitarist.'

'Yes.'

'And…well, does Keith Richards have an allotment. Or Chuck Berry? Does Howlin' Wolf grow hollyhocks?'

Mrs Harrison sounded confused. 'I don't know. Does he?'

'I don't think so,' said Freda.

'Sorry, Boys, You Failed the Audition'

'No, well, perhaps not. I'll tell George you phoned.'

'Thank you.' She was about to put the phone down when she remembered why she'd phoned. 'Oh, yes. Miss New Brighton?'

Mrs Harrison's voice hardened. 'Well, I suppose George likes her. She's from Chester!'

Freda put the phone down. George had always been the deep Beatle, but...an allotment! Her grandfather had had an allotment. Nothing was turning out the way she'd expected. It had taken three years, but she was finally having to admit to herself that the Rolling Stones weren't just good. *Satisfaction* and *The Last Time* were two of the best records of all time. But George Harrison and hollyhocks...!

Her route home took her around the back of Sefton Park where a travelling fair had occupied a levelled bombsite for a week every summer for most of her life. As a little girl she'd looked forward to it, and as a young teenager, without much pocket money to spend, she'd gone just to hang about and listen to the records.

On this evening she had intended to walk on past it, but the siren sound of the Four Tops couldn't be denied. Making her way across the dried, rutted mud she leant against the barrier surrounding the dodgems arena and watched long-haired boys, in their brightly-coloured shirts, showing off in front of leggy girls, as they crashed and bashed their cars into each other.

That was when it hit her: properly hit her. The world had changed. A completely new generation had arrived, almost overnight. Only four years earlier everyone had been in drab colours, the girls in cardigans and the boys, at best, in grey Marks and Spencer jumpers. Now as she pictured those nights from 1962, it occurred to her that it was like watching an old black-and-white film.

But there was something else. That had been the Beatles' moment and they'd missed it. It was the future now and they weren't a part of it. And, therefore, neither was she. Her dad had been right.

It was time she faced facts. With every issue the circulation of her Ex-Beatles Newsletter was shrinking. Returned copies were being posted back to her, and she couldn't help but wonder how many more were just being discarded, the envelopes carrying them unopened and the money spent on stamps and stationery wasted.

Leaving the fair, she continued on home.

It was the sound of the Beach Boys on Radio Caroline North later that evening that made her mind up, when *God Only Knows* drifted into her bedroom through her open window from the house next door. The singing was so pure, that she sat back in her chair to listen.

When the record ended, she stared at her typewriter and a half-written newsletter for some minutes. Why was she still doing this? If the local fans were drifting away and the ex-Beatles didn't care, had never cared, why should she? A new generation had already taken over. Soon, if she dared even mention the Beatles in her now increasingly rare visits to the Cavern, kids would look at her as if she was one of those pathetic old women of forty who requested records by Engelbert Humperdink on *Housewives Choice*. Pulling the stencil on which she'd been working out of her typewriter, she inserted another.

'Dear Beatle Fans,' she wrote. *'With John now a local wit, George on his allotment when he isn't a last-minute replacement backing Dusty Springfield or Tom Jones, and Paul making a new life for himself at university, I realise I can't keep on looking over my shoulder. I don't know what Ringo's doing since he married Maureen, because he's disappeared, but I do know it's time for me to accept the inevitable and stop living in the past by writing these newsletters – which, if I'm honest, I know that very few of you still read.*

So, although I'm sorry to say goodbye, this is my final newsletter to you. I'm closing down the Ex-Beatles Fan Club. Thank you all for your help and support over the years. I've really appreciated it. Good luck. And, for the last time,

All the Beatle best.

Freda.'

As she finished writing, she felt her father's presence at her side.

'Are you all right, love?' he asked.

She sniffed back a tear. 'I'm fine, Dad. Thanks. Good night.'

'Good night. God bless,' he said and crept out.

A few minutes later she dried her tears, and put the stencil in her bag for copying at work the following day.

Chapter Nine

The bus was crowded and she had to stand on the platform at the back as it made its way into town. She was thinking, as she had been for half the night, of the terrible betrayal that she had decided upon, so she didn't see the fellow's face. But as the bus pulled away from some traffic lights, a young scally ran down the stairs from the top deck, and, snatching her bag, jumped off and disappeared down a back entry.

'Stop! Thief! Stop!' she cried, hanging on to the rail as the bus gathered speed. But neither the bus conductor nor the thief heard her.

Her boss was very sympathetic, and, being a lawyer, insisted that Freda went immediately to the police station to report the crime. This was, Freda, realised the first time she'd been in a police station, and she waited with some apprehension as a young officer took out a bank of forms, and wrote down her name and address.

'When a crime has been committed, we have to list the items taken,' he said gravely as he bent over his desk. 'So, what was in the bag exactly?'

'Well, my purse...,' Freda began. 'There was two pounds, twelve and six in it. I was going to buy some nylons tonight on my way home. Then there were a couple of Luncheon Vouchers, some make-up, a comb, some lippy and a little mirror...'

'Anything else? A cheque book or...?'

Freda shook her head. 'Only a letter I'd intended copying and sending out when I got to work.'

'Did the letter contain any financial information, or anything of that nature?'

'No. It was just...well, I've been running an ex-Beatles Fan Club and...'

The young policeman stopped writing and looked up. '*I thought* I recognised the name. *Freda Kelly!* I'm on your mailing list.'

'Really? You, a policeman?'

'Why not?'

'I don't know. But you're not now, anyway. Not any more. I've closed the fan club down. It was in the letter that got nicked.'

The young officer stood straight up. 'You can't do that!' His voice echoed on the marble floor.

'What?'

'You're the keeper of the flame.'

'What flame?'

'The Beatles' flame.'

Freda almost smiled. 'I'm sorry, but you must have noticed. It's gone out.'

'That's because you've been doing it wrong.'

'Oh, thanks!' The boy policeman was insulting her now.

'No, what I mean is, instead of always going on about how great the Beatles were, and they were, you should be helping make them great again.'

'And how am I supposed to do that?'

'By getting them back together.'

'What? It isn't possible. They don't even talk to each other.'

'Have you ever tried to get them back together?'

'Well, no…'

'There you are then.'

'Where's there? Where am I?'

'You're here. In Liverpool. At your moment in history. Don't give up, Freda. The scally who nicked your bag with the letter did you a favour. Don't retype the letter. Don't close the Ex-Beatles Fan Club down. Get the Beatles back together.'

'I can't.'

'Yes, you can. If you try. It's your second chance. Get the Beatles back together and give them a second chance, too.'

'Get the Beatles back together!' It had never occurred to her. Was it even remotely possible, she wondered, as she made her way back to work. Had the snatching of her bag been a sign? She didn't believe in signs. But she didn't retype her fan club resignation letter either.

It was only when she was sitting on the stairs at a friend's twenty first birthday the next Saturday night as a boy called Chippy tried to unclip her bra, that she realised what she should do.

'Did you hear that what's-his-name has become a folk singer?' Chippy said as she pulled his hand away for the fourth time.

'Who's what's-his-name?' she said, readjusting her sweater again.

'You know, McCartney. Well, something like a folk singer. On his own, with a guitar...in London, in a basement in Soho. Me and the lads had a few bevvies and were wandering around after the Arsenal match and we heard some singing. So, we went in and there was McCartney sitting in a corner singing something about an easy game to play, which seemed about right as we'd just won. Everybody was talking and ignoring him, so we started shouting a bit of encouragement, you know, like, "sing I *Saw Her Standing There*, Paul". Remember when he used to do that one?'

Freda did remember. 'What happened next?'

'Sorry, Boys, You Failed the Audition'

'The manager sent these big blokes over and they threw us out,' said Chippy, and, picking up his bottle, went off to find a more negotiable bra clip.

Freda didn't mind. She was glad to get rid of him. But if Paul was singing and playing in public again…

'He's got his degree,' Mr McCartney told her proudly on the Monday morning when she phoned him. 'He was just trying to raise a bit of money before starting teaching.'

'Paul's going to be a teacher? Where?'

'Here. In Liverpool. He's got a job at a new school near Penny Lane. He's done very well.'

Yes, he had, hadn't he, Freda agreed. But, more importantly, Paul would be back in Liverpool. Permanently. The bobby fan had been right. It must have been a sign, after all. Sort of, anyway. He'd been quite nice looking, too – the young policeman.

Chapter Ten

'I'm sorry, Freda, but it seems to me that the ex-Beatles are perfectly happy *not* being together,' Brian Epstein told her over cucumber sandwiches at the Adelphi Hotel. It was the first time she'd been there and she was trying to remember to eat daintily in such a posh place. 'Though I've no idea what Ringo's up to.'

'But they're wasting their talents,' Freda protested. 'And that's criminal. A sin, really.'

'A sin?'

'Well, yes. It's like what Jesus said in the parable of the talents about the servant who buried what he was given instead of cashing it in or doing something useful with it. And how he was then "cast out into the darkness where there was much weeping and gnashing of teeth".' She wasn't sure about that bit, but it sounded about right. 'Don't you remember?'

'Actually, we didn't talk much about Jesus in the Epstein family,' Brian smiled.

'Didn't you?' Freda asked, astonished. 'I thought everybody did.'

'And, correct me if I'm wrong, but I'm pretty sure that Jesus wasn't talking about the talents involved in a two guitars, bass and drums rock and roll band.'

'Probably not. But the message was the same.'

Brian put a hand on hers. 'And so is mine. I'm sorry, Freda. Thanks for thinking of me, but trying to reunite four reluctant ex-Beatles isn't something for me. I suppose the truth is, I've outgrown them. Actually, I'm surprised that you haven't. There's more to life than pop music, you know.'

'Such as?'

'Well, lots of things. Bullfighting, for instance.'

'Bullfighting?'

'It's very exciting.'

'Really. You don't get to see much bullfighting in Liverpool.'

'There's more to life than Liverpool, too.'

'So people say,' Freda came back. 'But there's only one Mersey Tunnel, isn't there.' She didn't know why she said that. But it sounded like the sort of line that someone would say in a film.

It was no use, of course. There was no convincing him. It had probably never been about the music with Brian, she told herself, as she then listened as he told her about a bullfight he'd seen in Malaga. She should have known. He'd been the one who'd insisted the Beatles sing *The Sheik of Araby* at their Decca audition. It had been the most untypical song in their repertoire.

'Remember me to the boys, if you see them,' he told her as they said goodbye on the Adelphi steps. 'We had some good times.'

She promised him that she would and took his hand. He was always very polite, even when he was, in effect, telling her to get lost.

She couldn't hide her disappointment. Her father had been very impressed when she'd told him she'd been invited to tea at the Adelphi – something no-one in their family had ever been able to afford, but he wasn't surprised by Brian's lack of interest. 'You can't blame the man,' he said. 'He got his fingers burned with that lot once before.'

'Yes, I know. But it was as though he'd never really been a fan. Not in the way I was, anyway.'

'No, well, he's probably not a lunatic like you.'

That hurt. 'Oh, great!'

He put an arm around her. 'I'm sorry, love…' He hesitated. 'Perhaps…'

'Perhaps what?'

'Well, you know what they say.'

'No, what do they say?'

'God loves a tryer.'

'A tryer?'

'Yes. If you want something doing badly enough, you're best to try to do it yourself. If you really want to get the Beatles back together, you don't need Brian Epstein or anyone else. It's up to you.'

'I thought you hated the Beatles.'

'I do. At least, I did. But I love my daughter. I believe in her. And if, after all this time, she still believes in them, that's good enough for me.'

Freda looked at him. He never let her down. 'Thanks, Dad.'

'That's all right, love. Just as long as they don't bring any of their caterwauling around here.'

She wrote a new bulletin to the Ex-Beatles Fan Club a couple of nights later.

> *'Dear Fellow Fans.*
>
> *I've got a terrible confession to make. I came close to losing my faith recently and was seriously tempted to commit Beatlecide...which probably would get at least ten Hail Marys in confession. (That's a joke, by the way.)*
>
> *Anyway, I didn't, and I'm glad, because I've just seen a poster outside the Philharmonic pub saying that John is doing a 'happening' there tonight. I*

don't know what a 'happening' is either, so I think I'll just happen to go along and see if I can't talk some sense into him. I'll let you know how I get on. All the Beatle best for now.
Love
Freda'

Then, plucking up the courage, she added.

'PS. If you're reading this, PC 2018, thank you.'

She only just got there in time. Pushing through the smog of cigarette smoke in the saloon bar, she climbed the stairs. A group of trendies was already funnelling down the corridor, paying their two shillings each at the door, the men uniformly vague, studious and vacant looking with their beards and sandals, the girls intense with their daisy chain Alice bands and painted eyes. God, they look earnest, she thought, as feeling quite out of place, she looked for a chair.

At the top of the room a white bedsheet bearing the words '*LENNON-SENSE AND OTHER FOOLISHNESS*' scrawled across it in pink lipstick was hanging from one wall. Now, as people in front of her sat down, she could see John below it. He was sitting on a lavatory, his trousers around his ankles, as he waited to begin.

She was embarrassed. She'd never seen a man sitting on a lavatory before. What's more, he was wearing his awful horn-rimmed glasses, which he'd never done on stage at the Cavern. He probably thinks they make him look clever, she was just deciding, when the door was closed and John opened a notebook.

'*Once upon a rhyme,*' he began to read, '*there lived, in a roomy elephant's trunk, a loving couplet. He was an upstanding crotchet of a fellow with an enviable position in the pubic health department, and she was a quavering slip of a minuet with pursed lips and dainty hips.*

'"*Very pretty", neighbours would comment, and "catchy as a tune on the eye", as she whistled past on her way to her job attaching painted toenails to the alabaster earlobes of kangaroos.*'

Freda looked around nervously. John was talking gibberish, but the audience were all nodding and smiling, as though what he was saying was funny.

'*But heartbreak was only a Football Echo away from Nellie's trumpet of a dwelling place. For, unknown to Crotchet, a sly semibreve of a local bra had begun making overtures with bass motif to she of the dainty lips and pursed hips.*'

The audience laughed at that. Freda didn't.

'*Would he of the flared chords scale her heights? Would he leap an octave and remove her tights? Would he play a major or a minor chord on her knicker elastic? Would he? Would he? This Woody Woodpecker of a pesky pest...*'

On and on John went, and the sillier he got the more the audience laughed. Freda couldn't find anything to smile about.

'Well?' John demanded when, at last, he finished and the applause was stilled. Freda had been trying to get away, mortified by the whole performance, but he'd spotted her and caught up with her by the door.

'Well?' she repeated. 'Er...got a bit of a sniffle, actually. But not so bad, really,' she answered, deliberately misunderstanding. 'How are you, anyway?'

He smiled, understanding. 'It's surrealism, Freda. Don't you see?'

'It's what?'

'Surrealism. You know, like Jean Cocteau or Salvador Dali or Duchamp.'

'Duchamp?' she repeated, never having heard any of those names before.

'Yes. Duchamp!'

She was bewildered. 'You mean like *"Duchamp, duchamp...he's so fine...that handsome boy over there...the one with the wavy hair"*... The Crystals?'

John grinned. 'It was the The Chiffons, actually. But, yes, if you like... But without the backbeat.'

'Couldn't you have just sung *Roll Over Beethoven*?'

John looked surprised. 'Why would I do that?'

'You were brilliant at it.'

'Do you think so?'

'Absolutely.'

John pulled his horse's face, then shook his head.

'Nobody would want to hear me doing that now. It's been too long.'

'They would. Something like that, anyway.'

For a moment he looked wistful.

Had she touched a nerve, she wondered. 'How would you feel about getting the Beatles back...' she began, but just then a fellow with a pointy beard and a sugary voice intervened.

'Wonderful, John.'

John turned to the intruder. 'Really? It was only words you know. Gobbledogook...'

'Masking the subtlety of inner depth, I know,' Pointy Beard smarmed. 'Have you ever thought about writing slogans for advertisements? I have a feeling you might be rather good at it. Have you met Gregory? You must meet Gregory...'

'Well, all right, if you like.' John sounded unconvinced. 'I thought it was meaningless, meself, but....'

'...what about getting the Beatles back together?' Freda tried to intervene.

But it was too late. Putting an arm around his shoulder, Pointy Beard led John away into a coven of admirers. 'What a pity Ginsberg couldn't be here,' Freda heard the poseur say. 'He'd have been in fields of Elysium to have heard you tonight.'

The fields of where, Freda asked herself, as, giving up,

she became aware that John had now become the focus of a Juliette Gréco lookalike's attention. Clever girls had always gone for John, and John for them.

'You're right about the music,' came a voice alongside her. It belonged to Cynthia, John's wife. Freda hadn't noticed her in the crowd. Nobody ever seemed to notice Cynthia.

'Do you think so?'

'Absolutely. He sits for hours with his guitar writing songs, but usually never gets around to finishing them. And when he does, he's never satisfied. I don't think he knows what's good any more. What did you think of tonight, anyway?'

'Honest answer?'

Cynthia nodded.

'Well, it might be surrealism to John and that poncey lot he's now talking to. But to me it was all sails and no ship.'

Cynthia chuckled. 'I still read your newsletter, you know.'

'Really?' Freda was flattered. 'And John?'

Cynthia nodded. 'John first.'

'No?'

'Yes. Always.'

'In that case,' Freda said. 'You wouldn't, by any chance, know where I could find Ringo, would you?'

Chapter Eleven

She took the bus to Formby the next Saturday afternoon. Up the coast seven miles north of Liverpool, once a village it was now more of a little dormitory town. Getting off at the war memorial, as Cynthia had advised, she headed for the sea, making her way down a lane through the pine woods.

'You can't miss it,' Cynthia had said of Ringo's house. But she nearly did.

It was a grand, mock timbered mansion of a place just where the trees gave way to the sandhills. In the drive stood a brand-new silver E-type Jaguar alongside an equally shining powder blue Ford Capri.

This isn't it, she thought. It's miles too posh. But, as she was about to retrace her steps, the front door opened and Ringo appeared. He was wearing orange trousers and a kaftan covered in marigolds. With a droopy moustache, he looked very peculiar, but he grinned when he saw her. Then, glancing quickly from left to right to make sure that she was alone, he put his hands up in surrender.

'All right. You found me. I'll come quietly,' he joked.

'Is this your house?' Freda asked.

'Yes.'

'And the upstairs, too?' The place was big enough to house three or four families.

'And the garden and the swimming pool round the back,' he said, and he gestured towards a wide rear lawn behind a small mountain of rhododendrons.

'I've never known anyone have a house as big as this.'

'Until we bought it, neither had Maureen and me.'

'But…it must have cost a fortune. I didn't think Butlins paid their entertainers as well as this.'

Ringo laughed: 'They don't.'

'So…?'

'How could I afford it. Sorry, Freda. If I told you, you'd only write it in your silly Ex-Beatles Newsletter.'

'I wouldn't. Not if you asked me not to. And it isn't silly, anyway.'

'Well, if it gets out, I'll tell on you.'

'There's nothing to tell on me. I wish there was.' A thought crossed Freda's mind. 'You weren't one of the Great Train Robbers, were you? One that got away with all the money?'

Ringo looked at her. 'Do I look like a Great Train Robber?'

'Well, in certain lights… With that moustache.'

'My eight draws came up.'

'What?'

'The Treble Chance. I won the pools while me and Maureen were on our honeymoon in Prestatyn.'

'I don't believe it.'

'That's up to you. But it's true and it's a secret. I put my cross in the "no publicity" box. I was lucky'

'You were always lucky, Ringo.'

'If you like.'

Hanging around his neck, was what looked like a set of rosary beads. 'I didn't know you were a Catholic,' Freda said.

'What? I'm not,' he said, then realised what she was looking at. "These are worry beads. We've just come back from a holiday in San Francisco. Everyone's wearing them there. They'll catch on here soon. Why've you come?'

That worry beads would ever become fashionable in Liverpool seemed very unlikely to Freda, but, rather than argue, she got to the point of her visit. 'What would you say if the Beatles got back together and asked you to rejoin them?' she asked.

Ringo looked perplexed. 'The Beatles? I can't answer philosophical questions like that. I've got enough to do worrying about how I'm going to invest all my money. It isn't easy being rich, you know.'

'I bet it's easier than being poor,' said Freda.

That amused the drummer, and, inviting her into his Cape Canaveral of a kitchen, Maureen made a pot of tea and got out a packet of marshmallows. Then Ringo drove Freda back into Liverpool in his E-type.

This is how dolly girls must feel all the time, Freda thought, as the Jaguar raced back into the city. It must be nice to be a dolly girl sometimes.

Her father was standing over his upturned old bike in the back garden when she got home, the inner-tube immersed in a bowl of water as he searched for a puncture.

'He's a millionaire, you say,' was his only comment as she told him about Ringo's new house. 'I always said there's no justice in his world.'

'Oh, come on, Dad. He's really nice.'

'Nice, he may be. But that doesn't make it any the less true. I'm a nice fella, as well, so I'm told. But I'm not a millionaire, and never will be. Anyway, the police are after you.'

'What?'

'While you were out a young constable called round. Said he was just doing a follow-up report and wanted to make sure you were alright after the mugging.'

'Oh, is that all,' she said as nonchalantly as she could manage.

'And to thank you for mentioning him in your newsletter.'

She didn't think she blushed. 'Oh. That was just…'

'Yes?'

'Polite reciprocity,' she ended.

'Well, that's one way of putting it. He seemed a nice enough young fella. Said his name was Joe. PC Joe. Got a good, steady job, too…'

'So have I.'

'With a pension.' And, amused, her father pushed the tyre's inner tube back into the water and watched the stream of bubbles rise to the surface.

She caught up with George the next Saturday afternoon while he was deadheading the roses at his allotment. He's become very handsome now, she thought when she spotted him. With his hair long and wavy, he looked a bit like Jesus in his miracle working period – or perhaps the way a rock star does on the cover of his second album. Unfortunately, he hadn't made his first album yet.

'Why would any of us want to go backwards?' he answered when she put the big question to him.

'I'm sorry?'

He explained. 'Life's journey is forward, Freda. Like these roses. I plant them, they grow and bloom. Then they wither and die. That was what happened to the Beatles.'

Freda didn't know much about life's journeys, but her uncle had a greenhouse, so she did know a bit about flowers.

'Perhaps what the Beatles needed was some manure,' she said.

George stubbed his cigarette out in the soft soil. He was in a very deep mood today. 'If you've come to make jokes, I've got the greenfly to spray.'

'I'm not joking,' she said quickly. 'What I meant was that if you planted your rose bush in bad soil and in a place where it didn't get any sun it wouldn't do very well, would it.'

George carried on de-heading.

'But if you tried it somewhere else, like over there in the sunshine, and put some fertiliser around its roots, it might get a new start and be covered in rosebuds next year.'

George stopped clipping.

'It could be the same with the Beatles. Perhaps they just didn't get enough of the spotlight and help at the right time, and never got a chance to flower.'

'You've grown up, Freda.'

She was about to say 'So have you…' But just then a yellow Mini drew up on the other side of the fence. With a honking of its horn, a tall bottle-blonde climbed out.

Taking care not to step on his sweet peas, George went to greet her.

Freda followed. 'Miss New Brighton?' she enquired.

'That was last year. She's just been crowned Miss Southport 1967.'

'Going up in the world,' Freda murmured.

George didn't hear. 'This is Freda,' he said by way of half an introduction to his fiancée, as she stood by the allotment gate, probably not wanting to come further in case she got her high heels muddy. 'I think she's going to ask me if I'd like to play with the Beatles again.'

'Sorry? Play with who?'

'The Beatles,' said George.

Miss Southport 1967 looked puzzled. 'Who are the Beatles?'

She wasn't joking. She really wasn't.

George winced. Freda saw him. He did. He winced.

PC Joe screwed up his face in disbelief. 'She said what?'

He'd been standing on the corner of Dale Street and Hatton Garden, when Freda had spotted him on her way to work. Would she be breaking the law if she spoke to him about anything other than police work while on duty, she'd wondered, as she'd approached. His smile had reassured her. Then she'd told him about Miss Southport.

'"Who are the Beatles?" What kind of girlfriend is that?' he asked.

'The fiancée kind,' Freda replied.

PC Joe shook his head. 'There's only one thing for it, Freda. You've got to go and see Paul.'

'I can't.'

'You have to. He's back in Liverpool now, isn't he?'

'Yes, but…'

'But what?'

'He's a teacher now.'

'So?'

'I always hated school. Teachers frightened me. They still do. The very thought of school gives me the shivers.'

'You'll have to be brave then. Think of it as a sort of trial by ordeal. You have to go, Freda. Only you can do it.'

She looked at him. He looked so tall and important in his constable's helmet. But, most of all, he looked so trusting. 'All right,' she said. 'I'll do my best.'

Chapter Twelve

Paul was waiting for her on the steps of St Patrick's comprehensive school after classes. Wearing his teacher's corduroy jacket, all grown up and responsible, and now growing a sort of beard, he didn't look particularly pleased to see her. A flutter of admiring seventeen-year-olds watched her jealously as he greeted her. They'd been almost, but not quite, giving him the eye.

'I know what you want. George phoned me,' he said, as he led her against a tide of children who were rushing noisily for the door. Then, going down a corridor, he showed her into the school music room. 'And the answer's "no".'

'Do I have to call you "sir" now, sir,' she tried a joke.

He ignored it. 'The Beatles are ancient history, Freda. I told you years ago. You're the only person still in love with them. It's unhealthy to be so obsessed after all this time.'

'Everyone in the world would have been in love with them if they'd heard them,' Freda countered.

'But they didn't. And they never will. If I were you, I'd find a new band to follow. There are lots around.'

'I don't want to follow another band.'

'No, well, I'm sorry, but I'm sure we were never as good as you thought we were. It's unhealthy the way you don't give up. We'd never have been what you wanted us to be.'

'You were and you would.'

He didn't answer, but, aggravated by her persistence, slumped down at a piano.

Hurt by his bluntness, Freda felt tears leaking into her eyes, and looked around the room so that he wouldn't notice. On a desk alongside the piano was a scattering of handwritten song lyrics. She recognised his neat writing from the pieces of paper she'd rescued from the floor of the Cavern's stage as souvenirs. 'Do you teach music now?' she asked.

'What...? Oh, no,' he said, and then reflected for a moment. 'I come in here every day after lessons because, like an idiot, I promised to write a musical for the senior school to put on. So, here I am, sitting here, seeing what turns up.'

'You're writing new songs, you mean?'

'You could call it that, I suppose.'

'A Paul McCartney musical?'

'If only...'

'What's it about?'

'Oh...the usual. Schoolboy meets schoolgirl and the problems most kids face in their teens. Love behind the blackboard, kisses in the bike shed. Parents not understanding. Teachers fancying each other, or resisting the temptations of the pretty girls in the sixth form. It's set here in Liverpool.'

'What's it called?'

'*Suburban Skies*. But...' He stopped.

'What?'

'It's hard work and the clock's ticking. I don't know if I can finish it in time...or even if I can do it at all.' He looked towards the door. 'So, if you don't mind...'

She ignored the hint. 'Can't the other teachers help you?'

He gave her a wan smile. 'They might if it was about football. But, no...' He stood up. 'Anyway, come on, I've got to get on...'

Freda remained sitting. 'All right, but, before I go, could you play me one of your new songs...for old time's sake?'

Paul sighed. 'Only if you promise you'll leave when I finish.'

'Cross my heart and hope to die.'

He turned back to the piano. 'Well, all right, there's this one that I think isn't too bad,' he said feeling his way to a couple of chords. 'It's about the bus stop down the road and all the people who live and work there who the kids see every day on their way to school ... a nurse selling poppies, and a barber and a fireman. That sort of thing.'

And, passing her a sheet of lyrics, he began to play and then sing. It was a jaunty little tune - something for a chorus, Freda imagined. He only had half the words, so he had to hum the missing bits, but she got the idea. It was nothing like anything he'd ever played at the Cavern, but it was, well...*exhilarating*.

'It's not quite finished...' he explained as he stopped playing.

She nodded and thanked him and was about to get up to go as she'd promised, when he began another song. This time it was about an old spinster and a priest who was darning his socks in the presbytery during the night.

She should have known, she thought. Paul had always been a born entertainer. Once started, there would be no stopping him now, and bits and pieces of other half-written tunes began tumbling out of him. There was a fragment about somebody's older sister who worked as a parking meter attendant, and another about a runaway girl and her worried parents; and, in between, all of them, snatches of boogie-woogie rock and roll.

She did leave, eventually. But she couldn't very well go straight home after that. Instead she got the bus into the centre of Liverpool and made her way to the Georgian terraces that stood on the hill between the two cathedrals. The house she wanted was one of the most dilapidated in the street, and stepping under a porch of crumbling stucco, she pressed a bell that was Sellotaped to the wall.

Cynthia Lennon, holding a silent four-year-old Julian by the hand, opened the door, surprised, but pleased to see her. 'He's in,' Cynthia said, and led her past an old pram up four uncarpeted, echoing flights of stairs to a top floor flat.

Freda looked around. It was a two-room home of whitewashed walls decorated with hand-painted flowers, threadbare armchairs bombed with gaily coloured cushions, and with records, books and Julian's toys scattered everywhere.

John was lying on an ancient double bed, an acoustic guitar across his chest, wearing a pair of round National Health glasses. The sleeve of Elvis's first album, with its pink and green lettering was stuck on the wall behind him, partly covering a patch of damp.

'Well, well, this is a nice surprise, isn't it,' John teased, mock gossipy when he saw her. 'I was just saying to Cyn, "wouldn't it be nice if good ol' Freda dropped in to talk about the old days", and, hey presto! Here you are. I must be psychic.'

'Actually, it's the new days I want to talk about,' Freda countered. 'I've been to see Paul, and...'

'You mean Paul, as in Paul McCartney, the teacher,

one-time bass player and occasional falsetto and singer of high harmony with a group called the Beatles? He used to do a very good Little Richard impersonation, I seem to remember.'

'Yes, well... he's writing songs for a school show and he'd like you to give him a hand.'

Taking off his glasses, John put down his guitar and glared at her. 'Does Paul know you're telling lies about him?' The gentle mocking was gone.

'I'm not. It isn't a lie if it's probably the truth.'

For a moment John hesitated as if considering the logic of that, and then said. 'Paul wouldn't send you begging to me.'

'All right, he didn't,' she said. 'But he's stuck. And there's no one else who can help him.'

'God, Freda. You just don't give up, do you!'

'I can't. If I give up no-one else will bother, and...'

'And...?'

'And...all right! If you want my opinion...' Her voice grew louder. 'You know and I know that you're throwing your talent away being a smart arse on the stage in front of a gang of pseuds.'

'What?'

'Yes. A smart arse, a Liverpudlian big mouth writing soft poems and drawing daft cartoons. You're better than that, John Lennon, and you know it.'

Suddenly John was smiling, his expression quite comical. 'Christ, Cyn, just listen to her! Here was me looking forward to a quiet night in, and then I get a tirade like this. She's worse than Mimi.'

'No-one's worse than Mimi, John,' Cynthia jibbed, and, picking up Julian, went into the kitchen to make some tea.

For several moments John stared at Freda, as if weighing up something in his mind. 'Do you really think I'm better than that?' he said at last.

'Don't you...?' she replied.

Dad was in the hall listening to someone on the telephone when she got home. They'd only just had a phone put in, and she'd been giving the number to everyone she knew.

'Oh, just a minute, she's just walked in,' she heard him say.

He turned to her, putting his hand over the mouthpiece. 'It's for you, love. It's that McCartney fella. He sounds a bit upset.' And, giving her the phone, he went into the kitchen and closed the door.

'Hello, Paul...?' she said nervously.

Paul wasn't just a bit upset. He was flaming. 'How dare you!' he shouted.

'How dare I what?'

'I'd *never, ever* ask John Lennon for help,' he shouted. 'Never! It's right what he said about you.'

There was more, much more. But Freda was hardly listening. Finally, Paul paused for breath.

'Do you mean John rang you?' she said.

'Yes. And we agreed. You're a real pest.'

She smiled and smiled. They were finally talking again – even if it only was about her.

Chapter Thirteen

Cynthia phoned her at work a few days later. She was very excited, and suggested they meet in the Kardomah in Stanley Street on the Saturday morning.

'It's just like it used to be. John and Paul working together again...' she said.

'...on Paul's musical?' Freda asked.

'Actually, it's more like a joint musical now.'

'Really! McCartney and Lennon? Like Rogers and Hammerstein?'

'Actually, I think it's Lennon and McCartney,' Cynthia corrected. 'The letter L coming before M.'

'Oh, I see.'

'It's as though all their ideas for songs were locked up inside them both for years. And now that they're together again, they're all coming rushing out.'

'I'd love to see them working,' Freda said.

'Well, as you started it, I'm sure, if you keep very quiet...you could be a fly on the wall when they're writing.

They're so busy, they'll probably hardly notice you. They never seem to notice me.'

And they hardly did notice, as, night after night, with Julian in bed, Freda and Cynthia sat at the back of the room as John and Paul faced each other with their guitars, cups of tea on the side and ciggies on the go, playing and singing head to head. Occasionally Paul would break off to scribble down lyrics on a sheet of Julian's drawing paper, and sometimes John would lose interest and pick up a newspaper for inspiration. And, with Freda's silent presence in the Lennons' flat simply accepted, the musical raced ahead.

Naturally, John's idea for the concert wasn't quite the same as Paul's. 'What if we change the story a bit?' he suggested one night.

'To what?' Paul wanted to know.

'Well, perhaps one of the kids is from a children's home like the one that was near us when I was living with Mimi.'

'And?' Paul pursued.

'Well, maybe his girlfriend is clever and wants to go to college and he's scared of losing her. So…'

'Go on.'

'…he murders her and keeps her head in a jar…'

'Under his bed?'

'By the door. The kids would love that,' John smiled.

'The headmaster and parents might not though,' was

'Sorry, Boys, You Failed the Audition'

all Paul said, and the idea was forgotten, although John's song about the children's home was kept in, along with one about a dream girl who came to stay.

Watching them work, fascinated Freda. For the last few years rock music had sounded very American, most hits being copies of Rolling Stones' r and b or Motown. But the songs John and Paul were coming up with were like nothing Freda had ever heard before, eccentric little stories about Liverpool life in all kinds of different styles and rhythms.

There was little conversation. Never were the old days, or indeed the past few years, discussed, nor were current news events much talked about, other than for John's occasional jokes. 'I see Mick Jagger's joined the Moonies,' he said during one break.

'I think you mean the Maharishi,' came back Paul.

'Do I? All right, well him or some other fakir who's after the Rolling Stones' money.'

'It's the price of fame,' Paul replied.

'Is it? Well, it's too expensive, if you ask me.'

Soon a word was added to the show's title, *Suburban Skies*.

'Shouldn't it be *Blue Suburban Skies*,' John suggested.

'Why?' asked Paul.

'Adds colour,' came the reply and they went back to work.

Occasionally, when they met at Paul's school, a pretty young teacher with an elfin cut and long bare legs would come and stand by Paul, listen for a while, and then leave again. She was, he said, Greta, the show's director, and would be conductor of the choir. 'But she really a biology teacher,' he added.

'I wish she'd teach me some biology,' returned John.

'Yes, she knows her stuff,' said Paul, and they carried on working.

Within a few weeks *Blue Suburban Skies* had songs, a slight but workable story and lots of eager young actors and singers learning their parts. But all was still not quite right. Freda couldn't be at the school rehearsals, as she had to be at work, but as the first night drew closer, she could see that Paul was becoming increasingly worried.

It came to a head in the Cracke, a pub near the Lennons' flat, one night, when Paul arrived in a state of despair. 'It's no use. It isn't going to work,' he said.

'But the kids are singing their hearts out.' That was Cynthia.

'Yes, they're great. But we've made the songs too complicated for the school band. The lad on the piano, Billy, is great, a real little Liberace, but some of the others can hardly handle their instruments, and this concert needs more than two chords and an occasional badly played Chuck Berry riff. We'll have to call it off.'

'You can't do that. Everyone's looking forward to it,'

Cynthia pursued.

Freda agreed. It was supposed to be a school concert. Did it really matter if the kids couldn't play very well? But when Paul was in one of his perfectionist moods it was best to keep quiet.

There was a long and thoughtful silence, finally broken by John. 'I suppose, you and me, Paul…we could help out a bit. You on bass, me on guitar, hiding behind the stage or underneath it, playing along with the band, only with us amped up louder, out of sight and drowning them. No-one need know.'

Freda looked at John. He was smiling at the very idea.

Paul nodded thoughtfully. 'That might work, but it'll take more than us two. We'll need, at the very least, a drummer who can keep time, and another guitar…'

Freda was already on her way out of the pub.

'You mean, you're asking me to play in a school band?' On the line from London, George sounded incredulous.

'With John and Paul,' Freda said, sitting on the stairs at home. 'No-one will ever realise it's you.'

There was a silence. Then: 'Freda, I'd like to help, but…I can't.'

'Is it because of Miss Southport?'

'Oh no,' George said quickly. 'No. She's…you know…'

'Yes. I do. I noticed. So…?'

'Well, I think I should stick around down here.'

'In London?'

'Yes. There's a rumour that the Rolling Stones might be on the look out for a new guitarist, and...'

'The Rolling Stones!' Even Freda sense the derision in her voice.

'Yes, Brian Jones keeps missing sessions, and Mick and Keith are getting fed up. So there might be an opening for someone else.'

Quite apart from her irritation that George should speak so familiarly of Jagger and Richards, Freda couldn't believe what she was hearing. 'I don't understand,' she said.

'What do you mean?'

'Well, why would you want to play with the Rolling Stones, when you could be playing with the Beatles?'

George almost laughed. 'Freda, the Rolling Stones are a world-famous group. They sell millions of records. Whereas the Beatles...'

'...are the Beatles.'

There was a long, long silence.

'Hello?'

No answer.

'Hello, George?'

Then, finally: 'Oh, well, all right. Just so long as they let me do one of my own songs this time.'

'Sorry, Boys, You Failed the Audition'

She hadn't been to the Cavern recently, so she was surprised when she phoned Ringo and Maureen told her that she would probably find him there. Making her way down into the basement, she found herself smiling. It was like going home.

Ringo was standing by himself in the centre of the club, a little man, staring around at the arches. 'Well, aren't you going to congratulate me?' he asked.

'Congratulate you on what?'

'On how I invested my pools win.'

'I don't know. How did you invest it?'

'I bought this place.'

'What? You've bought the *Cavern*?'

'Not just the club. The entire warehouse. If I hadn't the council were going to knock it down and turn it into car park.'

'No. How could they?'

'Well, they can't now. I thought I might turn the top floors into a hairdressing and beauty salon, with perhaps a nice steak house on the ground floor.'

Freda stared at him. 'You know, Ringo, you never cease to amaze me.'

'I never cease to amaze myself,' he grinned.

She knew the answer to her next question, but she had to ask it. 'So, will you?'

'Of course, I bloody will.'

Chapter Fourteen

It almost made her feel nostalgic for the smell of classrooms, dry books and wet wellies, as she entered the school hall and threaded her way between blazered children, embarrassed but pleased to be escorting their parents to their seats. So, for a moment or two, she paused to watch the school band and choir, giggling with excitement, as they took their places on the stage.

Her path then took her through a door at one end of the hall, and behind the stage. The four musicians were already there, waiting to play together, along with a physics teacher called Harold who was in charge of balancing the sound.

'Good to see you again, Freda,' former road manager Neil said, putting out a hand to welcome her. He was now doing very well in his career as an accountant, but tonight was special, he explained. So, he and his former assistant Big Mal, who had gone back to work putting in telephones for the Post Office after the Beatles had broken up, were always going to be there to help if they were needed.

'Sorry, Boys, You Failed the Audition'

It obviously wouldn't be quite the Beatles reunion Freda had so often dreamed about, and crouched together in secret, the group actually looked nervous, something they'd never been in their Cavern days. But she could see, too, that glint of anticipating a challenge. It would be a big night for them, too, she realised.

At five minutes after seven thirty, the school hall went dark and quiet. Peeping through the curtain that hid them, Paul put his hand up and signalled to Greta, the biology teacher who was conducting. The Beatles were ready.

They all waited. Then a series of chords from Billy, the boy pianist, filled the hall. And, as the choir began to sing about the barber, the fireman and the pretty nurse selling poppies from a tray, the school band began to play and the unseen Beatles to help them.

Bent over their instruments in the darkness as they secretly accompanied and embellished the children's music, the Beatles were invisible to the audience. But, almost immediately, Freda felt tears flooding her eyes, and she had to raise her head and blink to control herself.

She'd done it. No-one on the other side of the curtain, none of the children or parents or teachers would have understood, maybe not even the Beatles themselves. But this was her moment, too. The song that they were playing, and that the school choir was singing, seemed to say it all. It was about Liverpool and its people. She thought of her father, and how he'd wished her luck as she'd left the house that evening, and about PC Joe who'd insisted that she didn't give up. He'd so wanted to be present, and she'd asked Paul to get him a ticket. Unfortunately, he'd had to be on duty at Speke Airport.

The stars were, of course, the pupils on the stage, and the school band, who, as the cheers and applause rang out again and again, happily accepted the credit for guitar riffs and drum breaks that they weren't actually playing. This amused the Beatles enormously as they went from one song to another, one of George's called *Good Day Sunshine*, then one by John about it having been a hard day's night – whatever that meant. Song followed song and with every one the choir became more confident and the Beatles more elaborate in their playing.

The parents in the audience must have been astonished by the hitherto unrecognised talents of their children. So, when the concert ended, they immediately joined the pupils' demands for the popular young English teacher Mr McCartney, now a playwright, composer and musical director, to take a bow.

This Paul quickly did, thanking pianist Billy, Greta and physics teacher Harold and just about everyone at the school for their efforts, before his hand went up for quiet. 'But most of all I'd like to thank my co-writer and oldest friend, John Lennon, for making this show possible. I couldn't have done it without him and our other friends George Harrison and Ringo Starr.'

And, as the cast and audience applauded once more, and Paul gave a thumbs-up sign, George was heard to murmur to Ringo, 'No, you couldn't.'

'Well, I've heard worse groups,' John mused as the applause finally died and Paul returned backstage.

'Not a bad little band really,' agreed his co-writer.

'Those kids in the band will be the school stars forever...' Ringo reflected. 'Even though we cheated for them.'

'Cheating goes on all the time in London,' came in George, knowledgably. 'Groups go on *Top of the Pops* and mime playing to their own records when they didn't even play on them in the first place.'

'Really?' John said, admiringly of the new sophistication that George had acquired.

Freda smiled to herself. George was no longer the baby in the group.

They gave the school hall time to empty, before piling their equipment into the swishy Mercedes station wagon that Ringo was now driving. Then, as there was no room for her in the car, because Neil and Mal were in need of a lift, she caught the bus back into town. She didn't mind. That was how it had always been. She knew her place, and she'd done what she set out to do.

Her father met her in the hall as she opened the front door.

She nodded.

'Well done, love,' he said. 'Well done.'

He'd never understood, and never would, but he was, she knew, proud of her.

Chapter Fifteen

After the concert, her intention had been to leave it at that. She was successful in her job, and had just begun a part-time law degree. So, it wasn't as though she didn't have enough to do. But she couldn't forget the expressions on the Beatles' faces all those years earlier when Brian Epstein had told them they'd been turned down by Parlophone. So, when, over the next few weeks, word began to get around Liverpool that the Beatles were occasionally playing together again, just for the fun of it, and that their road managers, Neil and Big Mal, were with them, too, well, she just had to be there.

Then, one Sunday afternoon, as she was waiting in the otherwise empty Cavern for the Beatles to arrive to jam together, PC Joe pushed a paper bag bearing the NEMS logo into her hand. 'Happy birthday,' he said.

Freda hadn't heard him come in. 'But it isn't my birthday?'

'No?' The young bobby was smiling. 'Well, never mind. If it was, this would be your present. Go on. Open it.'

'My dad always warned me about accepting presents from strange men,' she joked as, opening the bag, she withdrew a cardboard container. 'Sony cassette recorder,' she read on the package.

'You keep saying that it isn't fair that because the Beatles never made any records you can't take their music home...' PC Joe explained. 'Well, now you can.'

Freda stared at her present. 'Oh, my god! Thank you... thank you.' She'd read about these new Japanese cassette players in the papers, but had never seen one before. Eagerly she began separating the player from its packing. This had to be her best present ever. Starting today she would begin to compile recordings of all the Beatles' songs – like a curator in a museum. As for PC Joe...he really was lovely.

She began recording that very day. It was 1968, a friendly, unrushed time with no expectations for anyone, just a solicitor's secretary watching and recording four old friends as they made music together. And, as the following weeks went by, and Paul continued teaching while John published a book of short stories – albeit only locally, George began to spend more and more time in Liverpool, having given up his dreams of joining the Rolling Stones. As for Ringo, he got on with building his business empire.

'Is that it, then?' Her father asked one night stopping in her room on his way to bed, as she sat listening to her recordings.

'What do you mean?'

'Well, don't you think you should let someone else hear them, too? Or do you want to keep them your own little secret?'

The following day she had some personal stationery printed with her name and address in firm business-like lettering. Then, putting together on a cassette eight of the best new Beatles' songs, mostly those written for the school musical, she sent it by registered post to CBS Records in London.

The cry of glee that she'd expected didn't come. Assuming that the package had been mislaid in the post, she wrote again, sending a replacement cassette. This time a short note arrived saying that CBS received several such cassettes every week and that 'the Beetles aren't quite what we're looking for'.

'London idiots who can't spell,' she told herself. But there were now plenty of other new record companies around. So, over the summer and autumn of 1968, as the Beatles continued to play together when they had time and George wasn't touring with some other group, she tried them all, one by one. There was Track, RCA, HMV, Island, Philips, Polydor, Columbia, Chrysalis and even Embassy, the Woolworths label. The few replies she received wished her luck elsewhere. A couple questioned the type of songs the Beatles were playing. They were, one producer wrote back, 'unlike anything else in the rock dominated charts, and would be therefore difficult to market. But thank you for sending us the cassette'.

She was astonished. That was the whole point of the Beatles. They *were* different. They always had been. Did record company people still have their ears stuffed with marshmallows, as John had said all those years ago?

In the end only one record company was left. It had represented the last resort for Brian Epstein, but, according to the *New Musical Express*, George Martin still worked there, albeit now as the senior producer. It was Parlophone.

His reply came in early December. 'I do indeed remember the Beatles,' he wrote. 'I would be very grateful if you could arrange for them to come down to London for another audition.'

Freda hesitated. Then she consulted PC Joe.

He shook his head. 'London was Brian Epstein's mistake,' he said.

She agreed and wrote back, insisting that George Martin come to Liverpool. If he was ever going to understand just how good the Beatles were, he had to see them at the Cavern.

For a couple of weeks there was no answer, and she began to wonder if she'd overplayed her hand. Then just before New Year she got a phone call from Mr Martin's secretary. 'Yes, Mr Martin and an assistant would be delighted to come to Liverpool,' the secretary told her. She sounded very posh.

Only at this point, nimbly forgetting to mention the rejections she'd received, did she tell John.

'You've done what?' John shouted. 'Jesus wept, Freda. The Beatles aren't even a professional band any more. We're just playing for fun.'

'Well, you'd better get professional. The audition's next week,' she said, and left it to him to tell the other Beatles.

> *'Dear Fans,*
>
> *I could see that they were only pretending to be angry,'* she wrote in her newsletter a few days later. *'And, since then, they've been rehearsing like mad every free minute they get, with George not even having time to tend his allotment.*
>
> *Anyway, it's all set. The Cavern, 1pm, on January 30, 1969. Please, everybody, come and support them, and bring any other fans you might know. I'll see you there.*
>
> *All the Beatle best.*
>
> *Freda.'*

That was the plan, she'd devised. A lunchtime gig would be just like the old, great days – even though it would involve Paul taking a couple of hours off school and George giving up a chance to be a stand-in with the Tremeloes in Huddersfield. Yes, the Tremeloes.

As the audition approached, Ringo was both excited

and nervous, which puzzled Freda, because he was usually very phlegmatic. Then she remembered. Pete Best had been the Beatles' drummer when they'd auditioned for Parlophone in 1962. Ringo had joined the group while they'd been waiting to hear the result. George Martin was said to have been unsure about Pete's playing. Would be now feel the same about Ringo?

Being a dependable employee, Freda went to work as normal on the day of the audition, her only request to her boss being that she took an early and extra long lunch break. And as the train from London pulled into Lime Street Station at 12.25, and George Martin and Geoff, his assistant, stepped down from their carriage, she was there, standing behind the barrier.

They could have walked, because it wasn't very far. But, keen to impress, Freda insisted on a taxi to Mathew Street, and then sat nervously next to the tall, well-spoken producer, trying to make small talk about his journey, wishing that she'd worn a different pair of shoes.

'And the audition is at...?' George Martin asked.

'The Cavern,' said Freda proudly.

'Which is...?'

'A club,' Freda replied, astonished that he didn't know. 'Actually, it's quite well known in Liverpool.' These Londoners still didn't know anything.

'Ah,' said the record producer.

'Sorry, Boys, You Failed the Audition'

Just then the taxi turned the corner into Mathew Street, and came to a sharp halt. Thousands of young people were blocking the road, and staring upwards.

George Martin peered at the mob. 'Is something going on?'

The answer was yes and no. Freda had hoped for a big audience, but hardly this many. But why weren't they already inside?

'There seems to be something happening on the roof,' George Martin said, putting his head back and shielding his eyes, as they got out of the taxi and made their way through the crowd.

Freda peered upwards. Neil was up there, and Big Mal, too, hauling a cable up the side of the building.

Just then, Ringo emerged from the door of the club. He looked embarrassed. 'Sorry, Freda. We've had a burst pipe. The Cavern's flooded. We can't go down there. It's even more hazardous than usual.'

Freda felt her heart curl. God, no! Why did it have to be today? 'But can't…?'

Ringo cut her off. 'Don't worry, we'll be doing the gig on the roof.'

'The roof! The Beatles on the roof!'

'Just make sure you don't step on a rat as you climb the stairs. See you up there.' And he was gone.

Freda turned to George Martin. 'I'm so sorry, Mr Martin. I'd no idea this was going to happen…'

George Martin was chuckling. 'Of course, you hadn't. But there's nothing to be sorry about. Shall we go?'

And, taking her arm, he led her up through the three floors of the warehouse past boxes of apples and oranges, cabbages and turnips and the odd rotting pomegranate.

Paul was waiting as they stepped out on to the roof. With his dark beard trimmed to long stubble, and his thick black hair combed back, he was wearing his teacher's dark, sensible suit with an open-necked, white shirt. Behind him John and George were ready at their microphones, guitars against their chests. At the back Ringo was hurrying to get behind his drums, as Mal and Neil finished plugging in the amps and speakers.

'So, Mr Martin, we meet again,' John nervously tried to joke, like a villain in a James Bond film.

In case George Martin didn't think John was funny, Paul quickly tried to cover for him. 'We'd hoped we'd be playing to an audience, Mr Martin…' he began to apologise, as he led the visitors to a row of chairs.

Mr Parlophone stopped him. 'I came to see and hear you, not the fans. What have you got for me?'

'Well, we thought we'd start with a new song…'

'So, let's hear it then.'

Touching the strings of his bass, Paul turned to his microphone. Then, with a nod over his shoulder to the others, he began to count them in. 'One, two, three, four…'

'Sorry, Boys, You Failed the Audition'

And with a thudding, throbbing of bass, guitars and drums the audition was under way, with a song Paul had only just finished with John's help, something about getting back to where they'd once belonged.

It was, thought Freda, a magical moment as the Beatles' guitars and voices carried off the Cavern roof and down to the crowds of waiting fans in the little street below. Nor did it stop there. Out the music went, right across Liverpool to astonished staff in the Liver Building offices, who, it was said, rushed to their windows to see what was happening, and then on along the docks. A news story in that night's *Liverpool Echo* reported that the music was so loud it could be heard all over central Liverpool, with students at the University coming out of their libraries and refectories to listen. Then there were children in school playgrounds who looked around in wonder, workers and passengers on the New Brighton ferry who tapped their feet, old people sitting on benches feeding the seagulls at the Pier Head who smiled to each other, and a young mother called Judy, on her way home from playgroup with her little boy, who thought about how she and her friend Freda used to go to the Cavern. And then there was the young policeman on his beat, who gazed up at the sky, and murmured, 'Thank you, Freda'.

Freda didn't need thanking. It was, she knew, the best half hour of her life. Nothing would ever beat this. And, as she stood there on the roof, she saw that the four Beatles were no longer the boys she'd known and thought about through all these years, but young men grinning to each other at little private jokes, displaying a new confidence and certainty.

Then, without warning, they stopped playing, and, from the streets below came the sound of thousands of hands clapping followed by a growing roar of applause.

Casually John leant into his microphone. 'Thank you very much,' he said in his mock music hall voice. 'We hoped we passed the audition.'

Freda looked at her guests from Parlophone. George Martin was smiling and smiling.

Oh, yes, his expression said, the Beatles had passed the audition.

Sitting in her bedroom that evening, Freda wrote her last newsletter:

> *'Dear Fellow Fans*
> *If you weren't there, you should have been. And if you were, thank you for coming.*
> *That's it for me. The Beatles won't need me anymore. I've done my bit. Thank you for all your help and patience over the years.*
> *For the very last time*
> *All the Beatle best.*
> *Love*
> *Freda'*

'Sorry, Boys, You Failed the Audition'

Pulling the stencil from her typewriter, she read through it once more before slipping it into her bag for copying the next morning. Then, checking her make-up in the mirror, she went downstairs, put on her best coat, kissed her father and hurried down the road to the bus stop.

PC Joe was waiting for her in town. She didn't want to be late.

Also by Ray Connolly

BEING JOHN LENNON – A RESTLESS LIFE

'This careful, thoughtful biography... For Connolly, it is Lennon's insecurities that are ultimately most revealing' - *The Sunday Times*

'Excellent... Connolly draws on his archive conversations with the Beatles to give a superb portrait of a dissatisfied star who couldn't stop reinventing himself' - *The Daily Telegraph*

'Brisk and eminently readable' - *The Times*

'A fascinating look at the life of John Lennon' - *Pittsburgh Post-Gazette*

'Well written and intelligent...Connolly's social and historical observations inform the book, adding depth and background' - *Sydney Morning Herald*

'Compulsively readable' -*The Irish Examiner*

SHADOWS ON A WALL

'Belongs on that select shelf of good literature about Hollywood' - *Washington Post*

'Satire...with a couple of black comedy surprises that would have delighted Alfred Hitchcock' - *San Francisco Chronicle*

'Probably the best novel about movie-making ever written' - *Sunday Express*

'Bright and blackly funny...the War And Peace of Hollywood novels' - *New York Library Journal*

'The best movie story I have ever read' - *Publishing News*

Printed in Great Britain
by Amazon